COINS
GLOB Man

nickelodeon

THE LOUD HOUSE

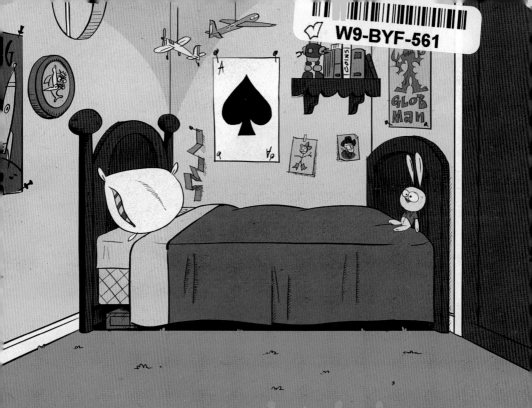

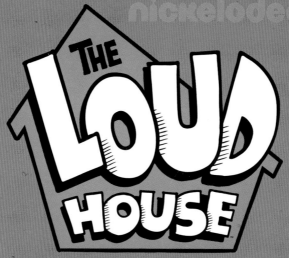

#4 FAMILY TREE

PAPERCUTZ
New York

nickelodeon GRAPHIC NOVELS AVAILABLE FROM PAPERCUTZ

THESE ALSO INCLUDE LOUD HOUSE STORIES!

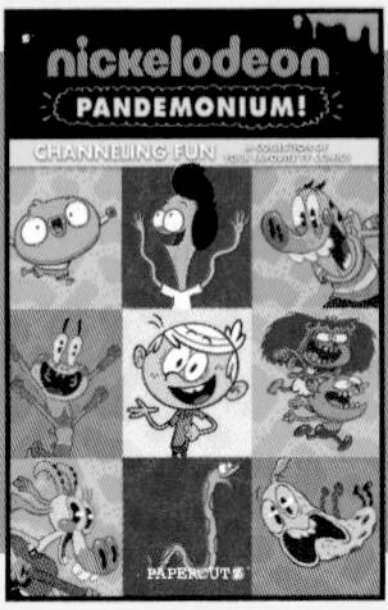
nickelodeon
PANDEMONIUM!
CHANNELING FUN
PAPERCUTZ

NICKELODEON PANDEMONIUM
#1
"Channeling Fun"

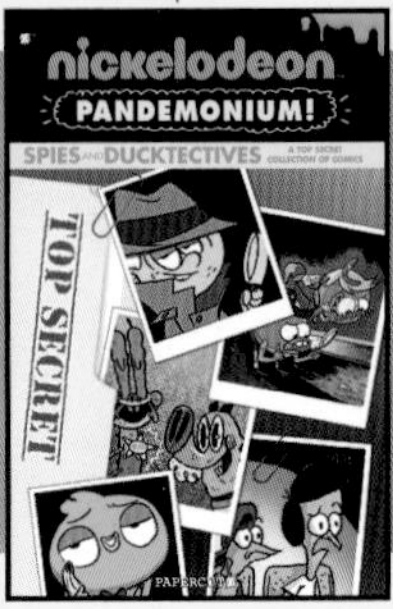
nickelodeon
PANDEMONIUM!
SPIES AND DUCKTECTIVES
TOP SECRET

NICKELODEON PANDEMONIUM
#2
"Spies and Ducktectives"

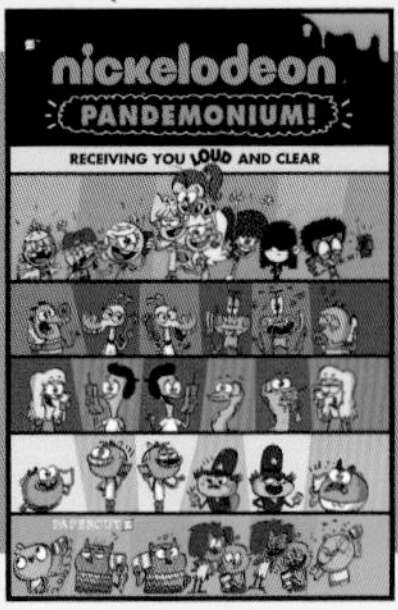
nickelodeon
PANDEMONIUM!
RECEIVING YOU LOUD AND CLEAR

NICKELODEON PANDEMONIUM
#3
"Receiving You Loud and Clear"

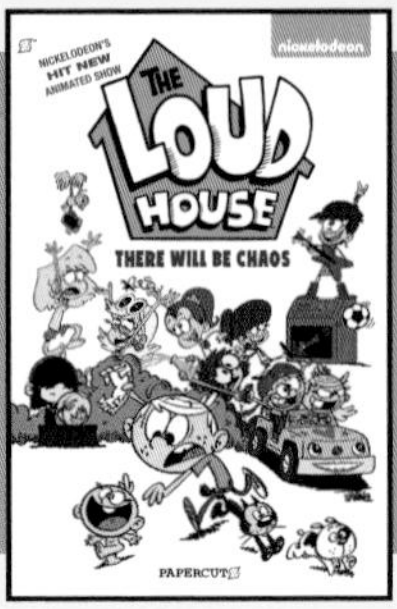
THE LOUD HOUSE
THERE WILL BE CHAOS
PAPERCUTZ

THE LOUD HOUSE
#1
"There Will Be Chaos"

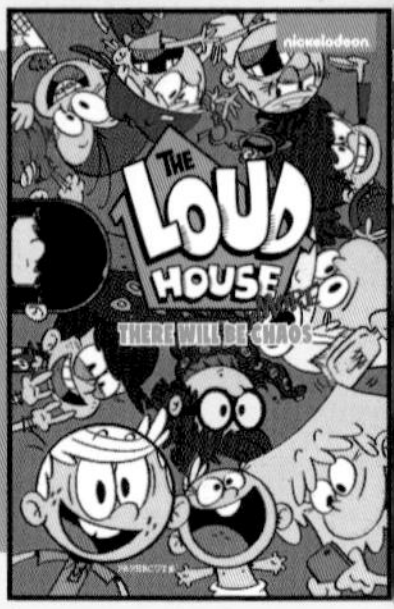
THE LOUD HOUSE

THE LOUD HOUSE
#2
"There Will Be More Chaos"

COMING SOON!

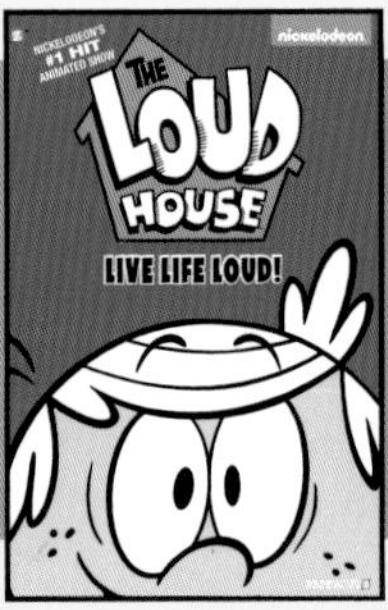
THE LOUD HOUSE
LIVE LIFE LOUD!

THE LOUD HOUSE
#3
"Live Life Loud!"

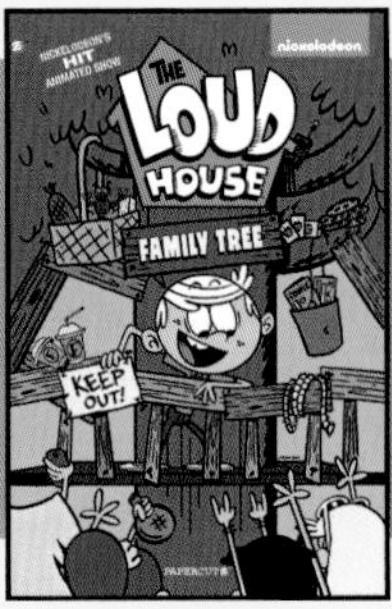
THE LOUD HOUSE
FAMILY TREE
KEEP OUT!

THE LOUD HOUSE
#4
"Family Tree"

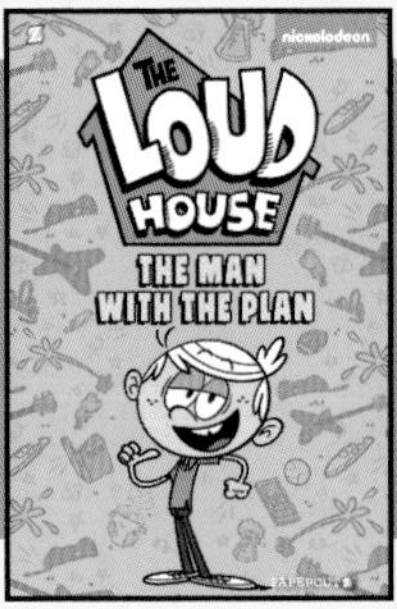
THE LOUD HOUSE
THE MAN WITH THE PLAN

THE LOUD HOUSE
#5
"The Man with the Plan"

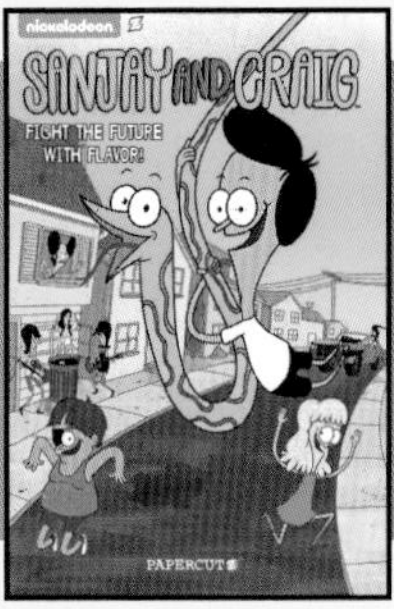
SANJAY AND CRAIG
FIGHT THE FUTURE WITH FLAVOR!
PAPERCUTZ

SANJAY AND CRAIG
#1
"Fight the Future with Flavor"

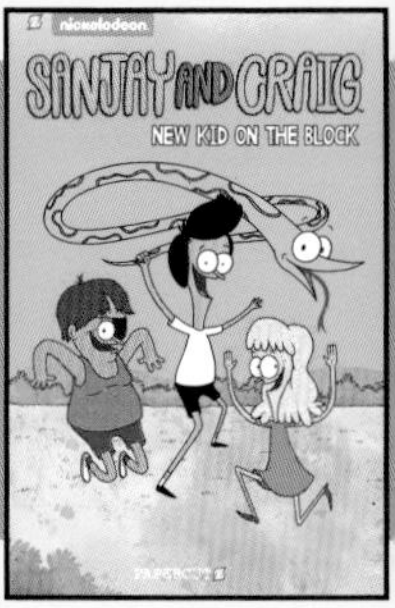
SANJAY AND CRAIG
NEW KID ON THE BLOCK

SANJAY AND CRAIG
#2
"New Kid on the Block"

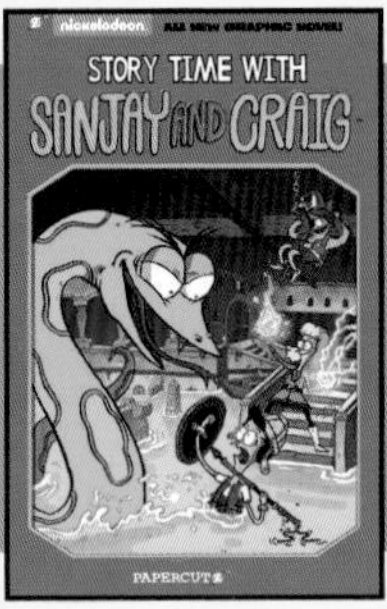
STORY TIME WITH
SANJAY AND CRAIG
PAPERCUTZ

SANJAY AND CRAIG
#3
"Story Time with Sanjay and Craig"

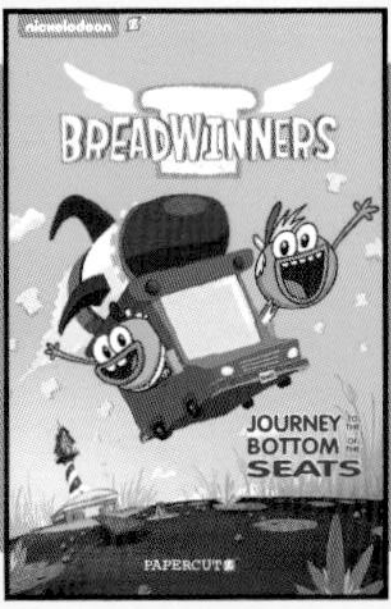
BREADWINNERS
JOURNEY TO THE BOTTOM OF THE SEATS
PAPERCUTZ

BREADWINNERS
#1
"Journey to the Bottom of the Seats"

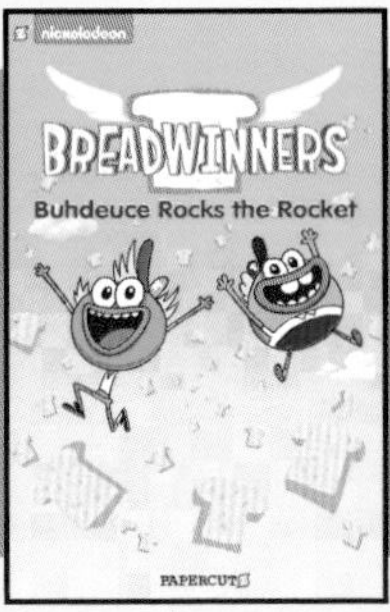
BREADWINNERS
Buhdeuce Rocks the Rocket
PAPERCUTZ

BREADWINNERS
#2
"Buhdeuce Rocks the Rocket"

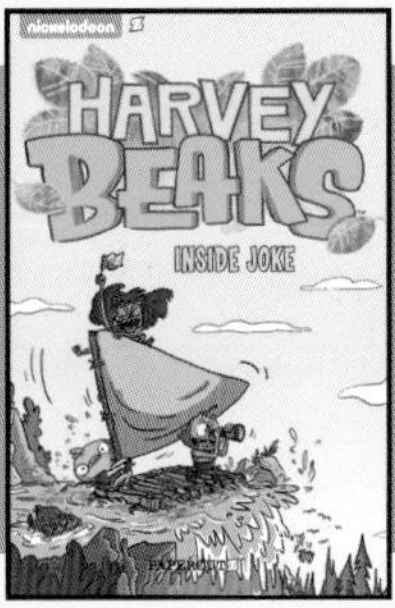
HARVEY BEAKS
INSIDE JOKE

HARVEY BEAKS
#1
"Inside Joke"

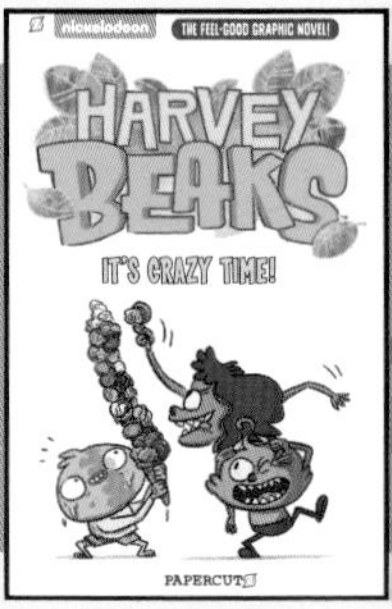
HARVEY BEAKS
IT'S CRAZY TIME!
PAPERCUTZ

HARVEY BEAKS
#2
"It's Crazy Time"

Nickelodeon graphic novels are available for $7.99 each in paperback, $12.99 each in hardcover. NICKELODEON PANDEMINIUM #3 is $8.99 each in paperback, $13.99 each in hardcover. Available from booksellers everywhere. You can also order online from Papercutz.com, or call 1-800-886-1223, Monday through Friday, 9-5 EST. MC, Visa, and AmEx accepted. To order by mail, please add $5.00 for postage and handling for the first book ordered, $1.00 for each additional book and make check payable to NBM Publishing. Send to: Papercutz, 160 Broadway, Suite 700, East Wing, New York, NY 10038.

Nickelodeon gr[redacted]er e-books are

THE LOUD HOUSE

#4 "FAMILY TREE"

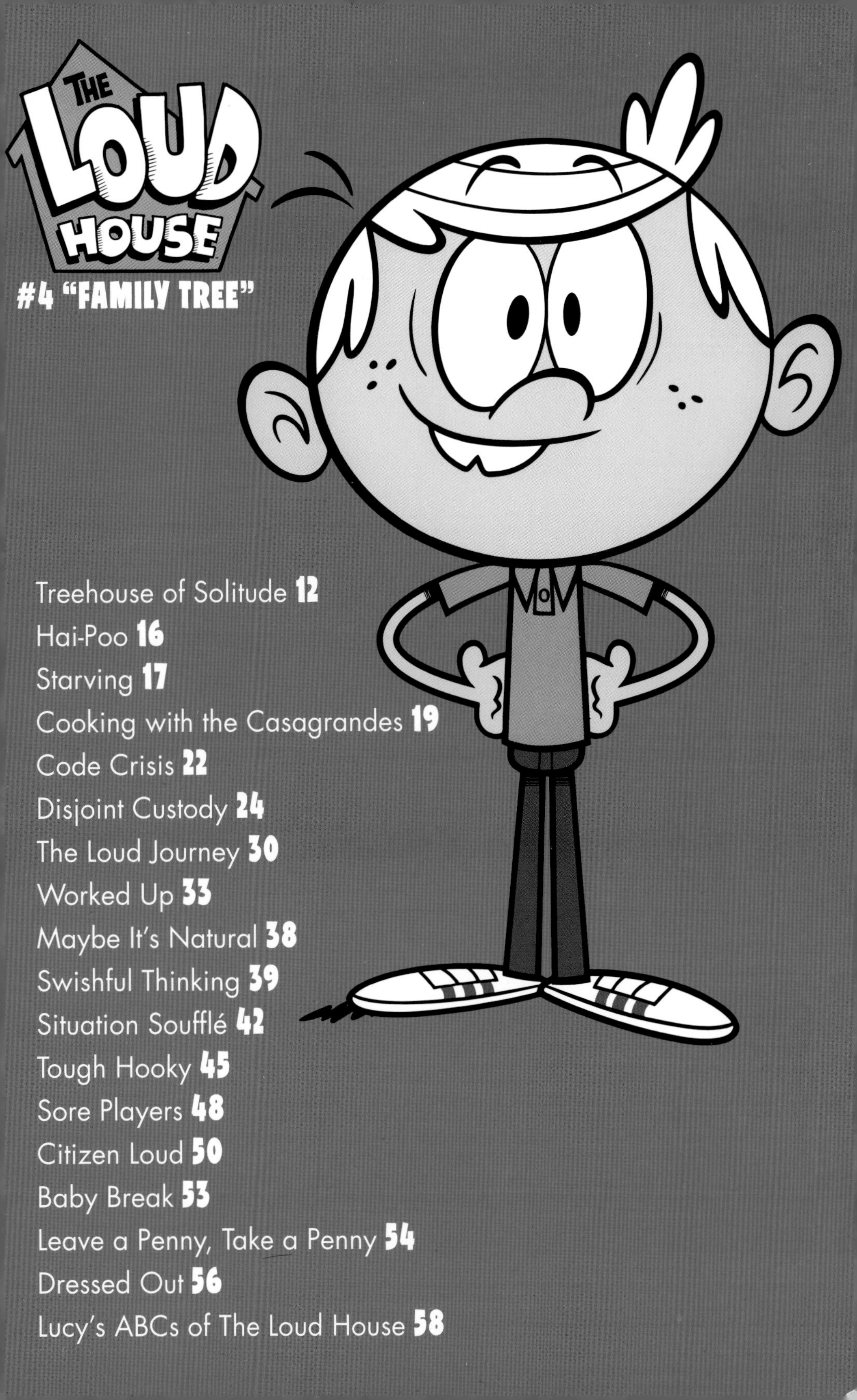

#4 "FAMILY TREE"

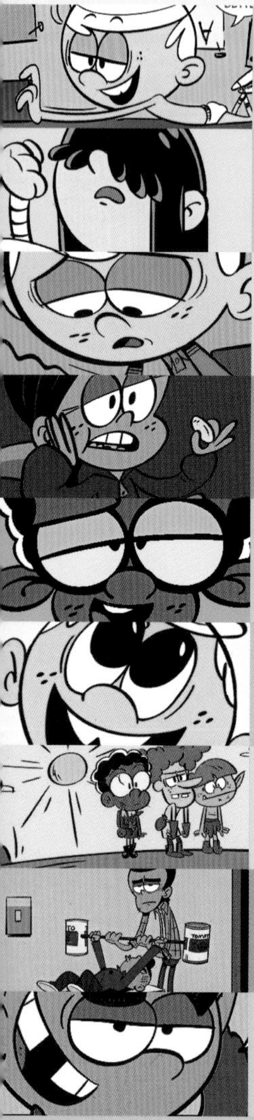

"TREEHOUSE OF SOLITUDE"
Sammie Crowley—Writer
David Teas—Artist, Letterer, Colorist

"SWISHFUL THINKING"
Andrew Brooks—Writer
Gabrielle Dolbey—Artist, Letterer, Colorist

"HAI-POO"
Jared Morgan
Writer, Artist, Letterer, Colorist

"SITUATION SOUFFLÉ"
Sammie Crowley—Writer
Ida Hem—Artist, Letterer
Hallie Wilson—Colorist

"STARVING"
Whitney Wetta—Writer
Ashley Kliment—Artist, Letterer, Colorist

"TOUGH HOOKY"
Jared Morgan
Writer, Artist, Letterer, Colorist

"COOKING WITH THE CASAGRANDES"
Gabrielle Dolbey
Writer, Artist, Letterer, Colorist

"SORE PLAYERS"
Diem Doan—Writer, Artist, Letterer
Gabrielle Dolbey—Colorist

"CODE CRISIS"
Whitney Wetta—Writer
Jordan Koch—Artist, Letterer, Colorist

"CITIZEN LOUD"
Angela Entzminger
Writer, Artist, Letterer, Colorist

"DISJOINT CUSTODY"
Sammie Crowley—Writer
Angela Entzminger—Artist, Letterer, Colorist

"BABY BREAK"
Diem Doan—Writer, Artist, Letterer
Gabrielle Dolbey—Colorist

"THE LOUD JOURNEY"
Diem Doan
Writer, Artist, Letterer, Colorist

"LEAVE A PENNY, TAKE A PENNY"
Jared Morgan
Writer, Artist, Letterer, Colorist

"WORKED UP"
Sammie Crowley & Whitney Wetta—Writers
Ida Hem—Artist, Letterer
Hallie Wilson—Colorist

"DRESSED OUT"
Andrew Brooks—Writer
Ashley Kliment—Artist, Letterer, Colorist

"MAYBE IT'S NATURAL"
Jared Morgan
Writer, Artist, Letterer, Colorist

"LUCY'S ABCs OF THE LOUD HOUSE"
Karla Sakas Shropshire—Writer
Kiernan Sjursen-Lien—Artist, Letterer
Amanda Rynda—Colorist

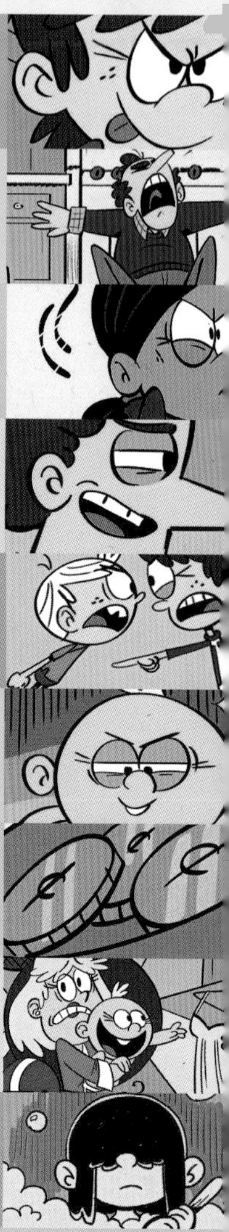

JORDAN KOCH—Cover Artist
JORDAN ROSATO—Endpapers
JAMES SALERNO—Sr. Art Director/Nickelodeon
DAWN GUZZO—Design
SEAN GANTKA, DANA CLUVERIUS, MOLLIE FREILICH—Special Thanks
JEFF WHITMAN—Editor
JOAN HILTY—Comics Editor/Nickelodeon
JIM SALICRUP
Editor-in-Chief

ISBN: 978-1-54580-005-8 paperback edition
ISBN: 978-1-54580-004-1 hardcover edition

Printed in India
July 2018

Distributed by Macmillan
First Printing

MEET THE LOUD FAMILY *and friends!*

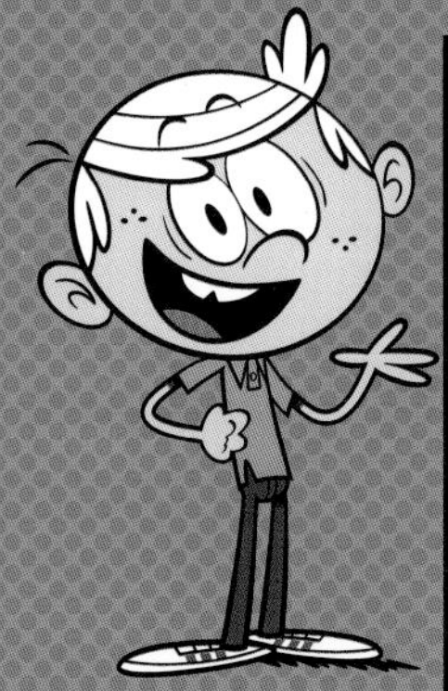

LINCOLN LOUD
THE MIDDLE CHILD (11)

At 11 years old, Lincoln is the middle child, with five older sisters and five younger sisters. He has learned that surviving the Loud household means staying a step ahead. He's the man with a plan, always coming up with a way to get what he wants or deal with a problem, even if things inevitably go wrong. Being the only boy comes with some perks. Lincoln gets his own room – even if it's just a converted linen closet. On the other hand, being the only boy also means he sometimes gets a little too much attention from his sisters. They mother him, tease him, and use him as the occasional lab rat or fashion show participant. Lincoln's sisters may drive him crazy, but he loves them and is always willing to help out if they need him.

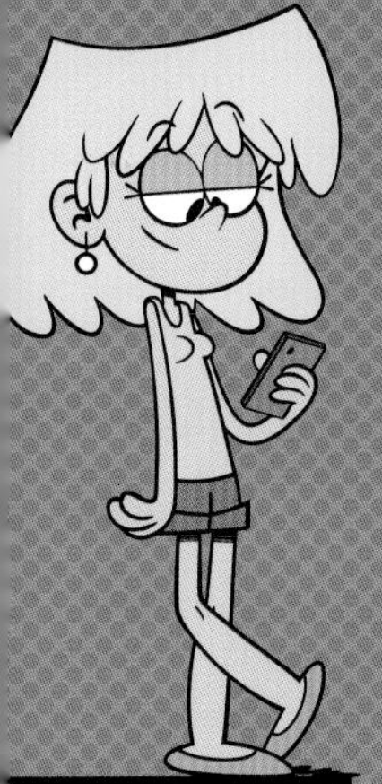

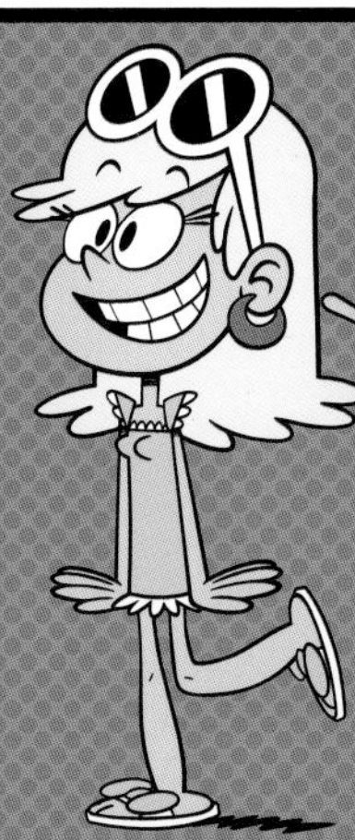

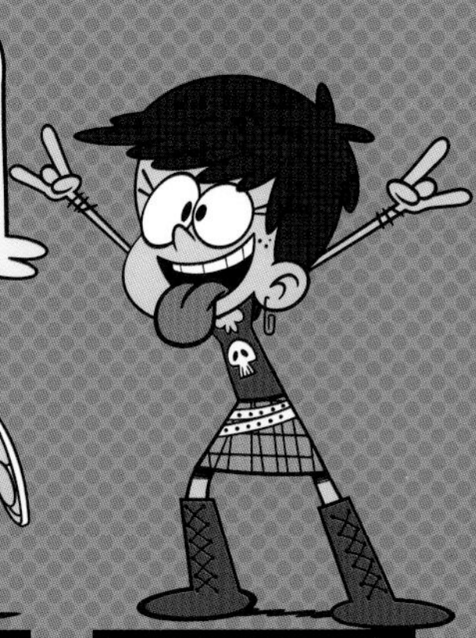

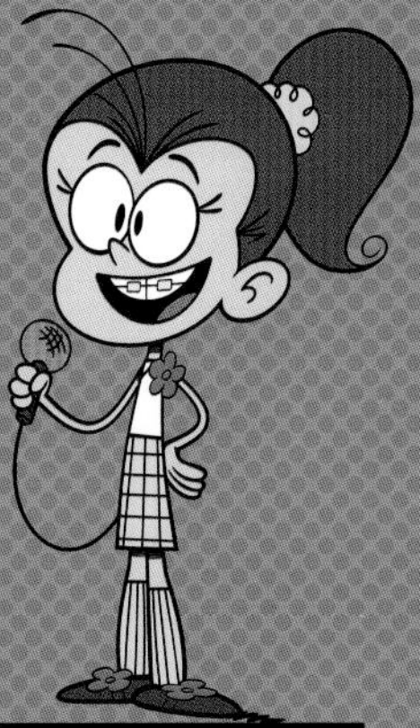

LORI LOUD
THE OLDEST (17)

As the first-born child of the Loud clan, Lori sees herself as the boss of all her siblings. She feels she's paved the way for them and deserves extra respect. Her signature traits are rolling her eyes, texting her boyfriend Bobby, and literally saying "literally" all the time. Because she's the oldest and most experienced sibling, Lori can be a great ally, so it pays to stay on her good side.

LENI LOUD
THE FASHIONISTA (16)

Leni spends most of her time designing outfits and accessorizing. She always falls for Luan's pranks, and sometimes walks into walls when she's talking (she's not great at doing two things at once). Leni might be flighty, but she's the sweetest of the Loud siblings and truly has a heart of gold (even though she's pretty sure it's a heart of blood).

LUNA LOUD
THE ROCK STAR (15)

Luna is loud, boisterous and freewheeling, and her energy is always cranked to 11. She thinks about music so much that she even talks in song lyrics. On the off-chance she doesn't have her guitar with her, everything can and will be turned into a musical instrument. You can always count on Luna to help out, and she'll do most anything you ask, as long as you're okay with her supplying a rocking guitar accompaniment.

LUAN LOUD
THE JOKESTER (14)

Luan's a standup comedienne who provides a nonstop barrage of silly puns. She's big on prop comedy too – squirting flowers and whoopee cushions – so you have to be on your toes whenever she's around. She loves to pull pranks and is a really good ventriloquist – she is often found doing bits with her dummy, Mr. Coconuts. Luan never lets anything get her down; to her, laughter IS the best medicine.

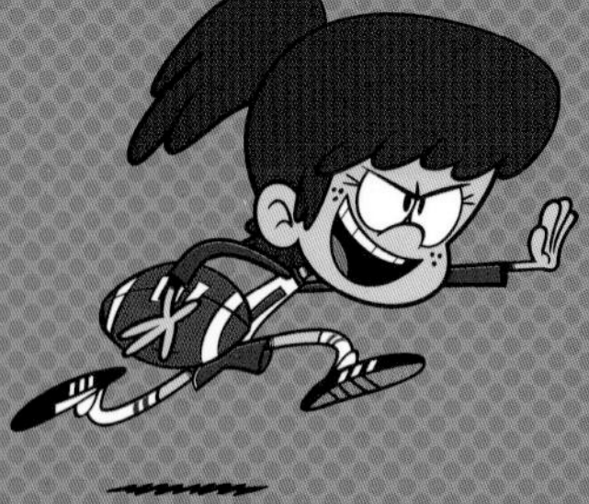

LYNN LOUD
THE ATHLETE (13)

Lynn is athletic and full of energy and is always looking for a teammate. With her, it's all sports all the time. She'll turn anything into a sport. Putting away eggs? Jump shot! Score! Cleaning up the eggs? Slap shot! Score! Lynn is very competitive, tends to be superstitious about her teams, and accepts almost any dare.

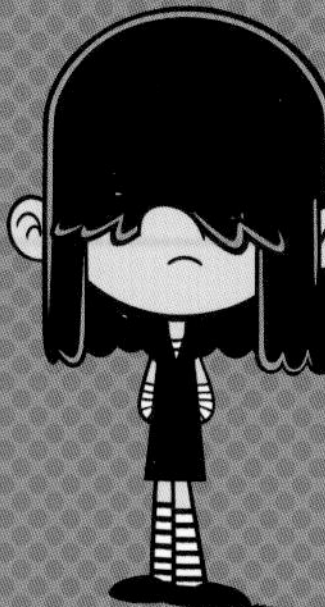

LUCY LOUD
THE EMO (8)

You can always count on Lucy to give the morbid point of view in any given situation. She is obsessed with all things spooky and dark – funerals, vampires, séances, and the like. She wears mostly black and writes moody poetry. She's usually quiet and keeps to herself. Lucy has a way of mysteriously appearing out of nowhere, and try as they might, her siblings never get used to this.

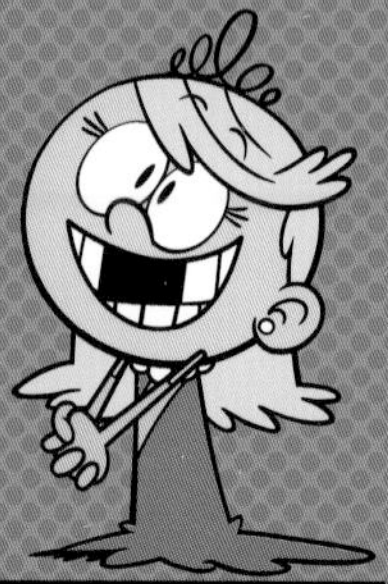

LOLA LOUD
THE BEAUTY QUEEN (6)

Lola could not be more different from her twin sister, Lana. She's a pageant powerhouse whose interests include glitter, photo shoots, and her own beautiful, beautiful face. But don't let her cute, gap-toothed smile fool you; underneath all the sugar and spice lurks a Machiavellian mastermind. Whatever Lola wants, Lola gets – or else. She's the eyes and ears of the household and never resists an opportunity to tattle on troublemakers. But if you stay on Lola's good side, you've got yourself a fierce ally – and a lifetime supply of free makeovers.

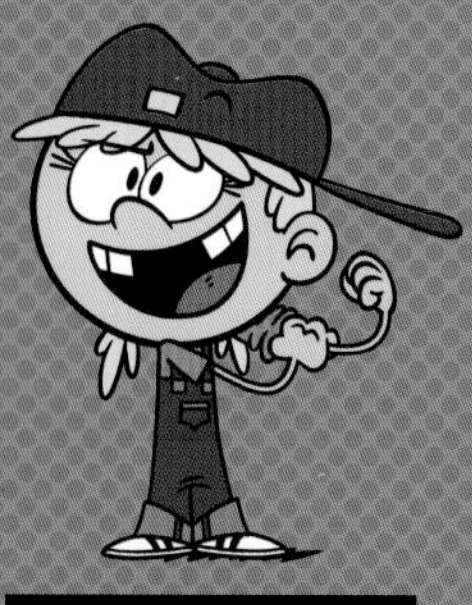

LANA LOUD
THE TOMBOY (6)

Lana is the rough-and-tumble sparkplug counterpart to her twin sister, Lola. She's all about reptiles, mud pies, and muffler repair. She's the resident Ms. Fix-it and is always ready to lend a hand – the dirtier the job, the better. Need your toilet unclogged? Snake fed? Back-zit popped? Lana's your gal. All she asks in return is a little A-B-C gum, or a handful of kibble (she often sneaks it from the dog bowl).

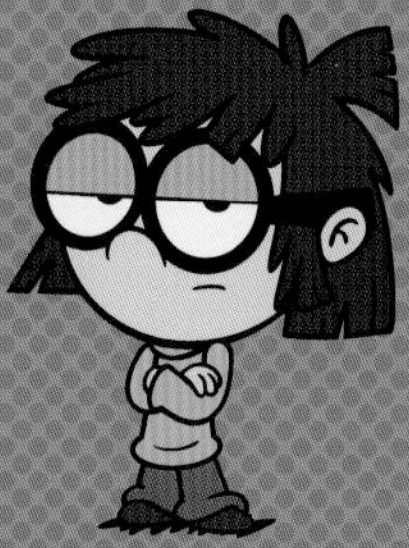

LISA LOUD
THE GENIUS (4)

Lisa is smarter than the rest of her siblings combined. She'll most likely be a rocket scientist, or a brain surgeon, or an evil genius who takes over the world. Lisa spends most of her time working in her lab (the family has gotten used to the explosions), and says her research leaves little time for frivolous human pursuits like "playing" or "getting haircuts." That said, she's always there to help with a homework question, or to explain why the sky is blue, or to point out the structural flaws in someone's pillow fort. Lisa says it's the least she can do for her favorite test subjects, er, siblings.

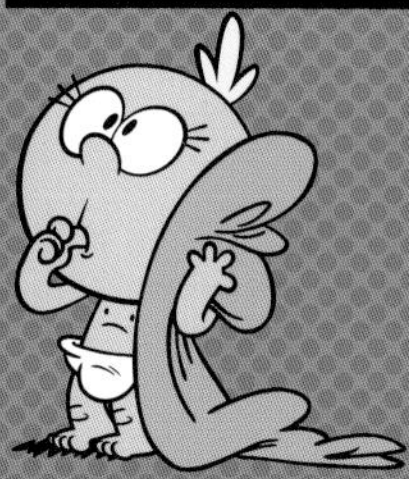

LILY LOUD
THE BABY (15 MONTHS)

Lily is a giggly, drooly, diaper-ditching free spirit, affectionately known as "the poop machine." You can't keep a nappy on this kid – she's like a teething Houdini. But even when Lily's running wild, dropping rancid diaper bombs, or drooling all over the remote, she always brings a smile to everyone's face (and a clothespin to their nose). Lily is everyone's favorite little buddy, and the whole family loves her unconditionally.

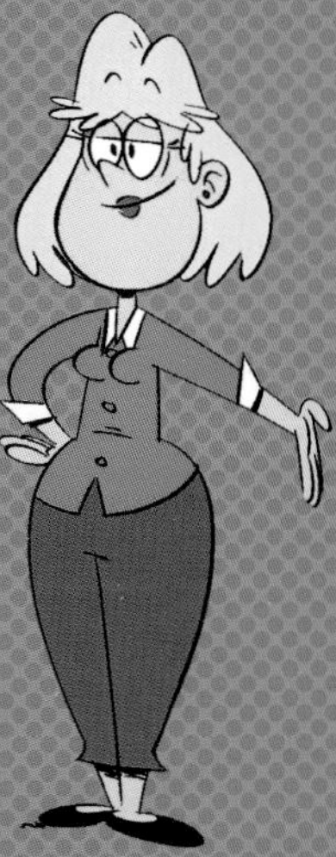

RITA LOUD

Mother to the eleven Loud kids, Mom (Rita Loud) wears many different hats. She's a chauffeur, homework-checker and barf-cleaner-upper all rolled into one. She's always there for her kids and ready to jump into action during a crisis, whether it's a fight between the twins or Leni's missing shoe. When she's not chasing the kids around or at her day job as a dental hygienist, Mom pursues her passion: writing. She also loves taking on house projects and is very handy with tools (guess that's where Lana gets it from). Between writing, working and being a mom, her days are always hectic but she wouldn't have it any other way.

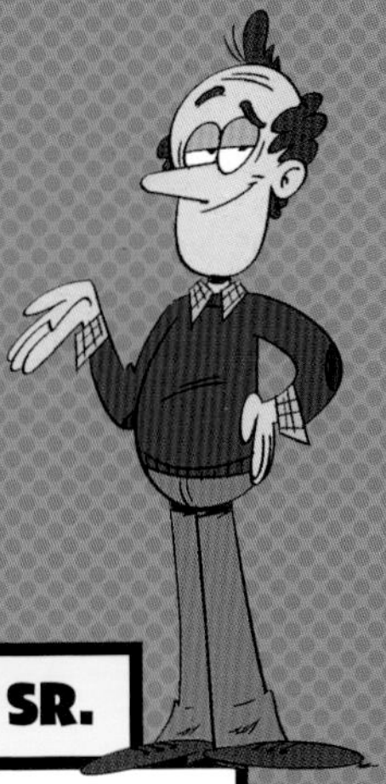

LYNN LOUD SR.

Dad (Lynn Loud Sr.) is a fun-loving, upbeat aspiring chef. A kid-at-heart, he's not above taking part in the kids' zany schemes. In addition to cooking, Dad loves his van, playing the cowbell and making puns. Before meeting Mom, Dad spent a semester in England and has been obsessed with British culture ever since – and sometimes "accidentally" slips into a British accent. When Dad's not wrangling the kids, he's pursuing his dream of opening his own restaurant where he hopes to make his "Lynn-sagnas" world-famous.

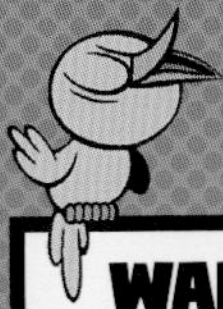

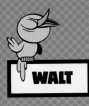

WALT

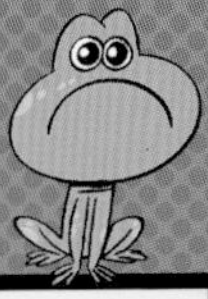

HOPS

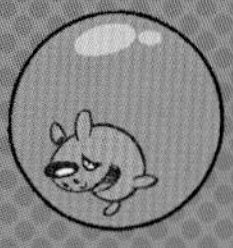

GEO

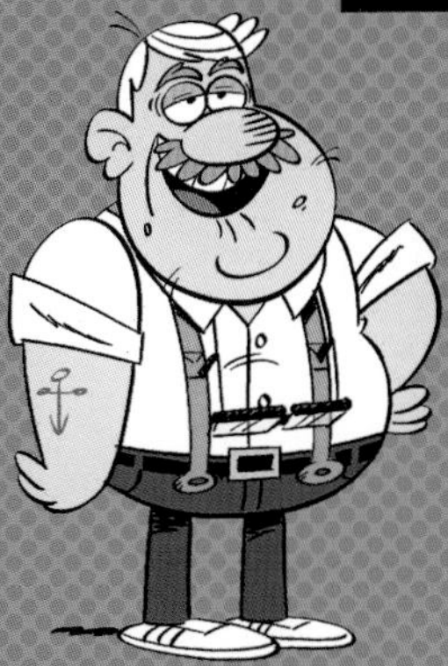

POP POP

Albert, Rita's father, currently lives at Sunset Canyon Retirement Community after dedicating his life to working in the military. Pop Pop spends his days dominating at shuffleboard, eating pudding and going on adventures with his pals Bernie, Scoots, and Seymour and his girlfriend, Myrtle. Pop Pop is upbeat, fun-loving and cherishes spending time with his grandchildren.

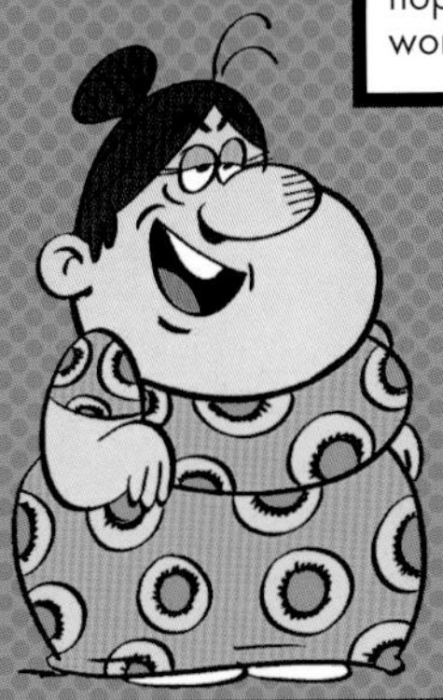

AUNT RUTH

Pop Pop's sister, Mom's Aunt and the Loud kids' Great Aunt. There's nothing Aunt Ruth loves more than her dozens of cats. Aunt Ruth also enjoys traveling and often does so with her cats in tow – most recently taking Mittens to Egypt. The kids dread visiting Aunt Ruth since she always tries to feed them expired food and requests foot massages from them.

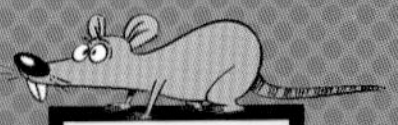

BITEY

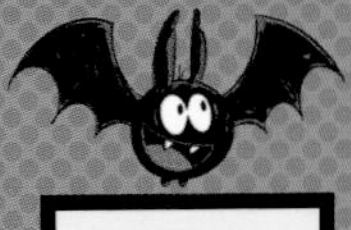

FANGS

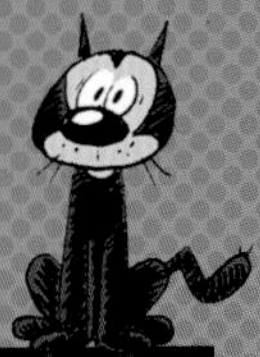

CLIFF

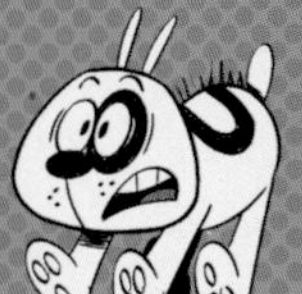

CHARLES

CLYDE McBRIDE
THE BEST FRIEND (11)

Clyde is Lincoln's partner in crime. He's always willing to go along with Lincoln's crazy schemes (even if he sees the flaws in them up front). Lincoln and Clyde are two peas in a pod and share pretty much all of the same tastes in movies, comics, TV shows, toys – you name it. As an only child, Clyde envies Lincoln – how cool would it be to always have siblings around to talk to? But since Clyde spends so much time at the Loud household, he's almost an honorary sibling anyway. He also has a major crush on Lori.

ZACH GURDLE

Zach is a self-admitted nerd who's obsessed with aliens and conspiracy theories. He lives between a freeway and a circus, so the chaos of the Loud House doesn't faze him. He and Rusty occasionally butt heads, but deep down, it's all love.

RUSTY SPOKES

Rusty is a self-proclaimed ladies' man who's always the first to dish out girl advice – even though he's never been on an actual date. His dad owns a suit rental service, so occasionally Rusty can hook the gang up with some dapper duds – just as long as no one gets anything dirty.

LIAM

Liam is an enthusiastic, sweet-natured farm boy full of down-home wisdom. He loves hanging out with his Mee Maw, wrestling his prize pig Virginia, and sharing his farm-to-table produce with the rest of the gang.

SAM SHARP

Sam, 15, is Luna's classmate and good friend, who Luna has a crush on. Sam is all about the music – she loves to play guitar and write and compose music. Her favorite genre is rock and roll but she appreciates all good tunes. Unlike Luna, Sam only has one brother, Simon, but she thinks even one sibling provides enough chaos for her.

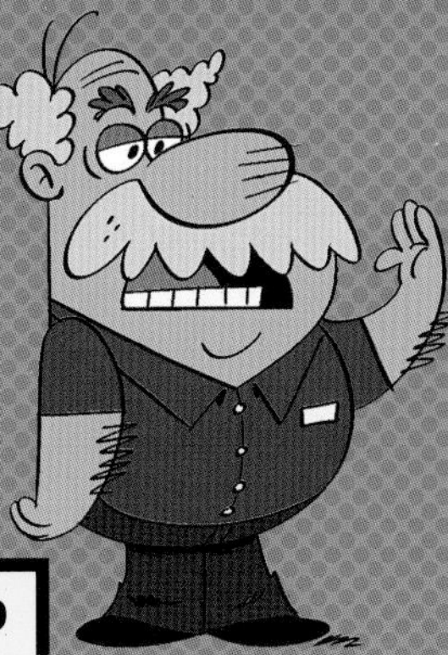

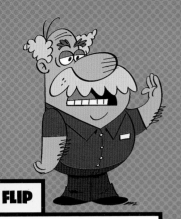

FLIP

The owner of Flip's Food & Fuel, the local convenience store. Flip has questionable business practices – he's been known to sell expired milk and stick his feet in the nacho cheese! When he's not selling Flippees, Flip loves fishing and also sponsors Lynn's rec basketball team.

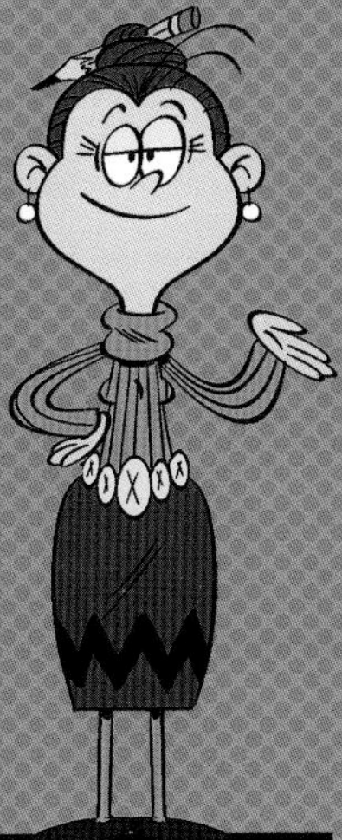

MRS. AGNES JOHNSON

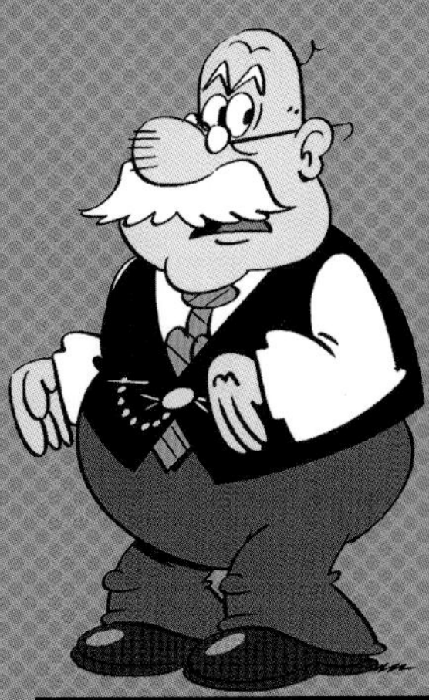

MR. BUD GROUSE

Mr. Grouse is the Louds's next-door-neighbor. The Louds often go to him for favors which he normally rejects – unless there's a chance for him to score one of Dad's famous Lynn-sagnas. Mr. Grouse loves gardening, relaxing in his recliner and keeping anything of the Louds's that flies into his yard (his catchphrase, after all, is "my yard, my property!").

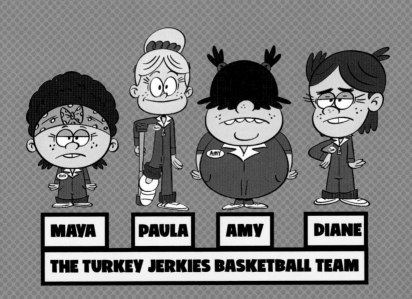

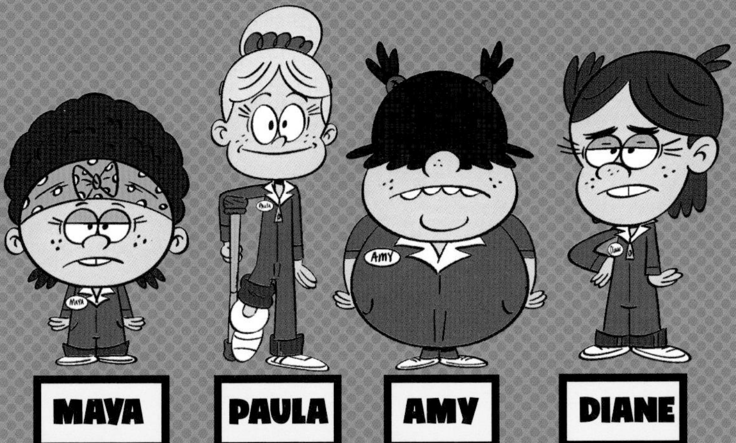
MAYA
PAULA
AMY
DIANE

MAYA | PAULA | AMY | DIANE

THE TURKEY JERKIES BASKETBALL TEAM

RONNIE ANNE SANTIAGO

Ronnie Anne's an independent spirit who's into skating, gaming and pranking. Strong-willed and a little gruff, she isn't into excessive displays of emotion. But don't be fooled – she has a sweet side, too, fostered by years of taking care of her mother and brother. And though her new extended family can be a little overwhelming, she appreciates how loving, caring, and fun they can be.

BOBBY SANTIAGO

Ronnie Anne's older brother, Bobby is a sweet, responsible, loyal high-school senior who works in the family's bodega. Bobby is very devoted to his family. He's Grandpa's right hand man and can't wait to one day take over the bodega for him. Bobby's a big kid and a bit of a klutz, which sometimes gets him into pickles, like locking himself in the freezer case. But he makes up for any work mishaps with his great customer skills – everyone in the neighborhood loves him.

MARIA CASAGRANDE SANTIAGO

She's the mother of Bobby and Ronnie Anne. A hardworking nurse, she doesn't get to spend a lot of time with her kids, but when she does she treasures it. Maria is calm and rational but often worries about whether she's doing enough for her kids. Maria, Bobby, and Ronnie Anne are a close-knit trio who were used to having only each other – until they moved in with their extended family.

HECTOR CASAGRANDE

He's the father of Carlos and Maria and the grandfather of six. The patriarch of the Casagrande Family, Hector wears the pants in the family (or at least thinks he does). He is the owner of the bodega on the ground floor of their apartment building and takes great pride in his work, his family, and being the unofficial "mayor" of the block. He's charismatic, friendly, and also a huge gossip (although he tries to deny it).

ROSA CASAGRANDE

She's the mother of Carlos and Maria and wife to Hector. Rosa is a gifted cook and has a sixth sense about knowing when anyone in her house is hungry. The wisest of the bunch, Rosa is really the head of the household but lets Hector think he is. She's spiritual and often tries to fix problems or illnesses with home remedies or potions. She's protective of all her family and at times can be a bit smothering.

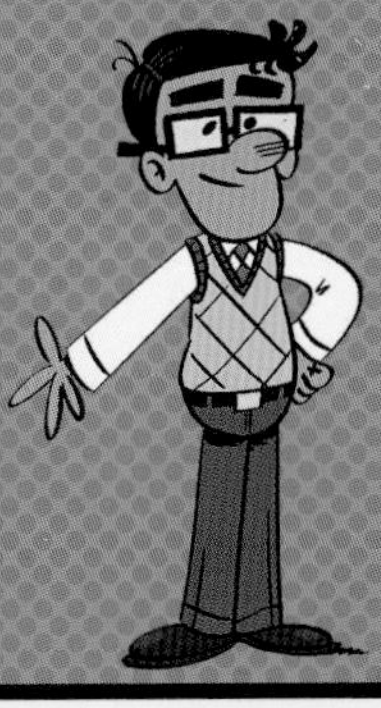

CARLOS CASAGRANDE

He's the father of four kids (Carlota, CJ, Carl, and Carlitos), husband of Frida, and brother of Maria. He's a professor of marine biology at a local college and always has his head in a book. He's a pretty easygoing guy compared to his sometimes overly emotional relatives. Carlos is pragmatic, a caring father, and loves to rattle off useless tidbits of information.

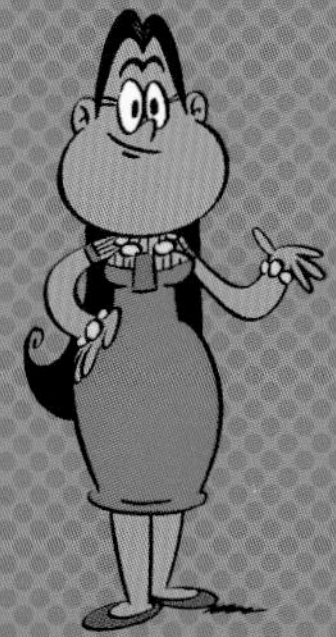

FRIDA PUGA CASAGRANDE

She's the mother to Carlota, CJ, Carl, and Carlitos and wife to Carlos. She's an artist-type, always taking photos of the family. She tends to cry when she's overcome with sadness, anger, happiness... basically, she cries a lot. She's excitable, game for fun, passionate, and loves her family more than anything. All she ever wants is for her entire family to be in the same room. But when that happens, all she can do is cry and take photos.

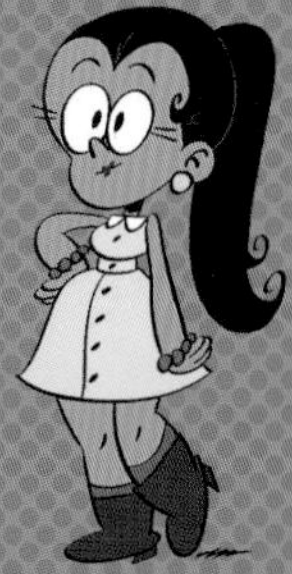

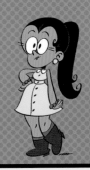

CARLOTA CASAGRANDE

The oldest child of Carlos and Frida. She's social, fun-loving, and desperately wants to be the big sister to Ronnie Anne. Carlota has a very distinctive vintage style, which she tries to share with Ronnie Anne, who couldn't be less interested.

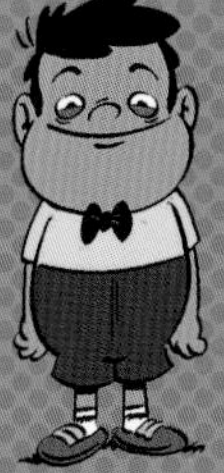

CJ (CARLOS JR.) CASAGRANDE

CJ was born with Down syndrome. He's the sunshine in everyone's life and always wants to play. He will often lighten the mood of a tense situation with his honest remarks. He adores Bobby and always wants to be around him (which is A-OK with Bobby, who sees CJ as a little brother). CJ asks to wear a bowtie every day no matter the occasion and is hardly ever without a smile on his face. He's definitely a glass-half-full kind of guy.

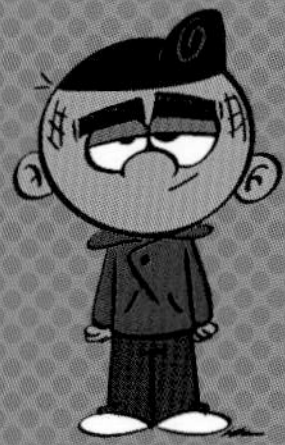

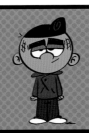

CARL CASAGRANDE

Carlino is 6 going on 30. He thinks of himself as a suave, romantic ladies' man. He's confident and outgoing. When he sees something he likes, he goes for it (even if it's Bobby's girlfriend, Lori). He cares about his appearance even more than Carlota and often uses her hair products (much to her chagrin). He hates to be reminded that he's only six and is emasculated whenever someone notices him snuggling his blankie or sucking his thumb. Carl is convinced that Bobby is his biggest rival and is always trying to beat Bobby (which Bobby is unaware of).

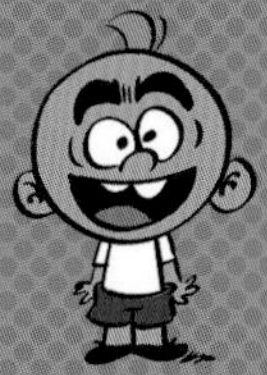

CARLITOS CASAGRANDE

The redheaded toddler who is always mimicking everyone's behavior, even the dog's. He's playful, rambunctious, and loves to play with the family pets.

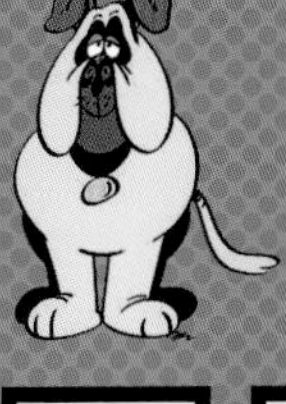

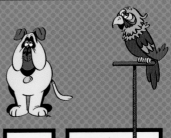

LALO

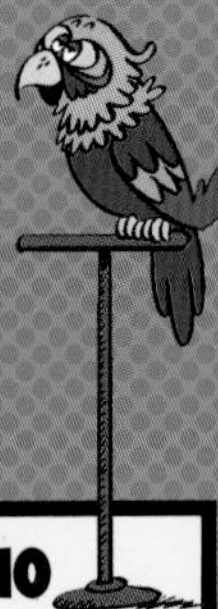

SERGIO

"TREEHOUSE OF SOLITUDE"

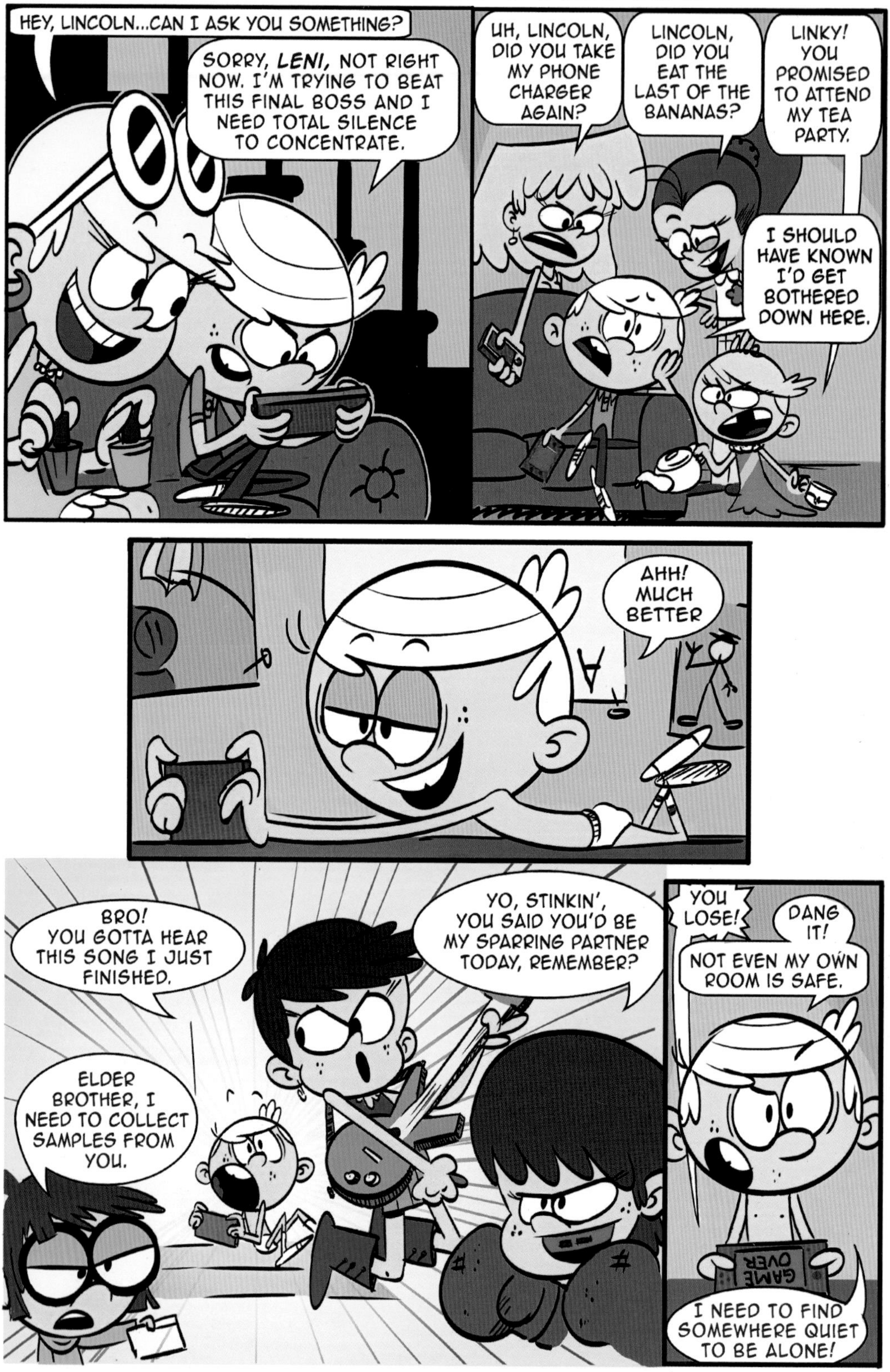
HEY, LINCOLN...CAN I ASK YOU SOMETHING?
SORRY, LENI, NOT RIGHT NOW. I'M TRYING TO BEAT THIS FINAL BOSS AND I NEED TOTAL SILENCE TO CONCENTRATE.
UH, LINCOLN, DID YOU TAKE MY PHONE CHARGER AGAIN?
LINCOLN, DID YOU EAT THE LAST OF THE BANANAS?
LINKY! YOU PROMISED TO ATTEND MY TEA PARTY.
I SHOULD HAVE KNOWN I'D GET BOTHERED DOWN HERE.
AHH! MUCH BETTER
BRO! YOU GOTTA HEAR THIS SONG I JUST FINISHED.
YO, STINKIN', YOU SAID YOU'D BE MY SPARRING PARTNER TODAY, REMEMBER?
ELDER BROTHER, I NEED TO COLLECT SAMPLES FROM YOU.
YOU LOSE!
DANG IT!
NOT EVEN MY OWN ROOM IS SAFE.
GAME OVER
I NEED TO FIND SOMEWHERE QUIET TO BE ALONE!

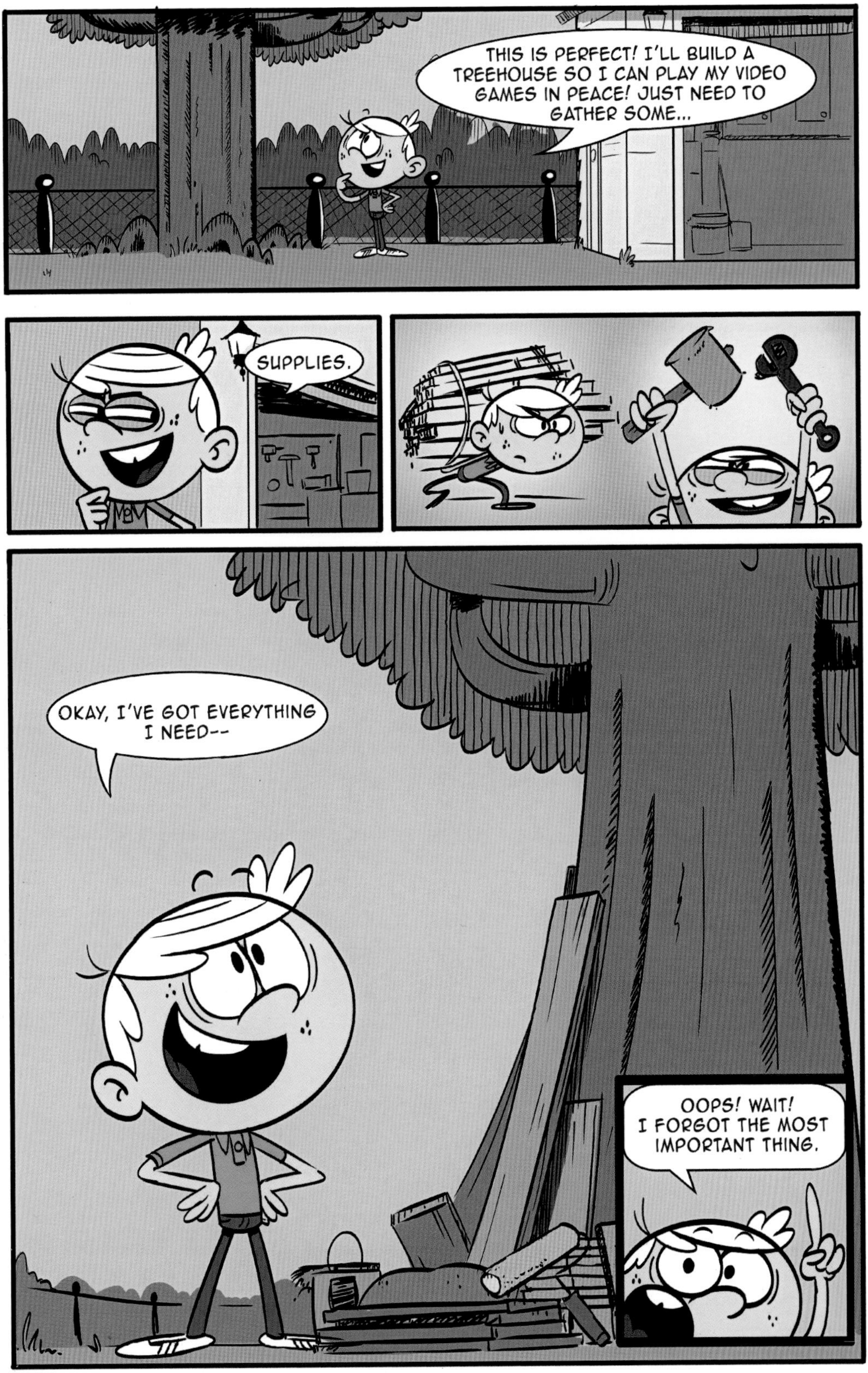
THIS IS PERFECT! I'LL BUILD A TREEHOUSE SO I CAN PLAY MY VIDEO GAMES IN PEACE! JUST NEED TO GATHER SOME...
SUPPLIES.
OKAY, I'VE GOT EVERYTHING I NEED--
OOPS! WAIT! I FORGOT THE MOST IMPORTANT THING.

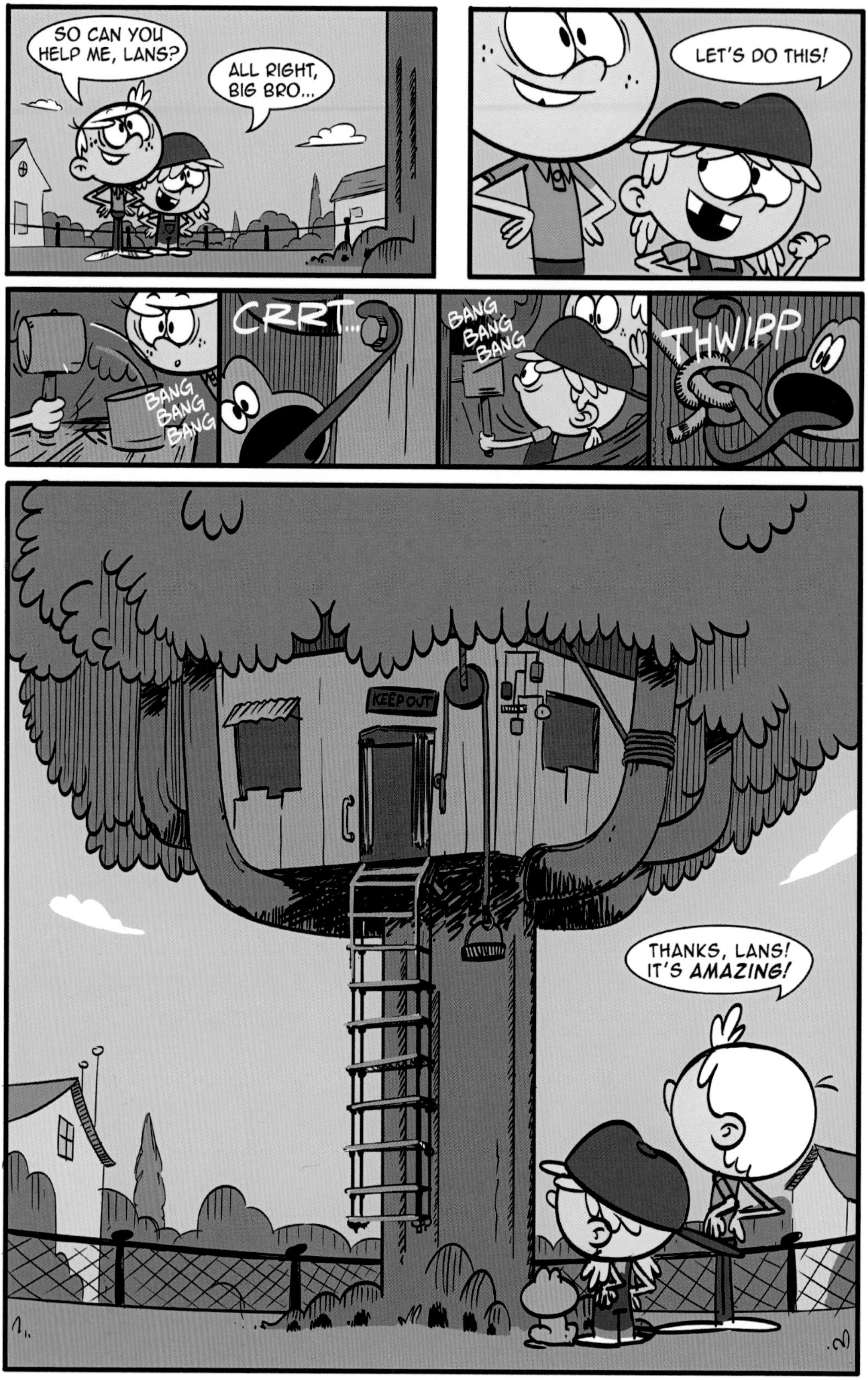
SO CAN YOU HELP ME, LANS?
ALL RIGHT, BIG BRO...
LET'S DO THIS!
BANG BANG BANG
CRRT...
BANG BANG BANG
THWIPP
KEEP OUT
THANKS, LANS! IT'S AMAZING!

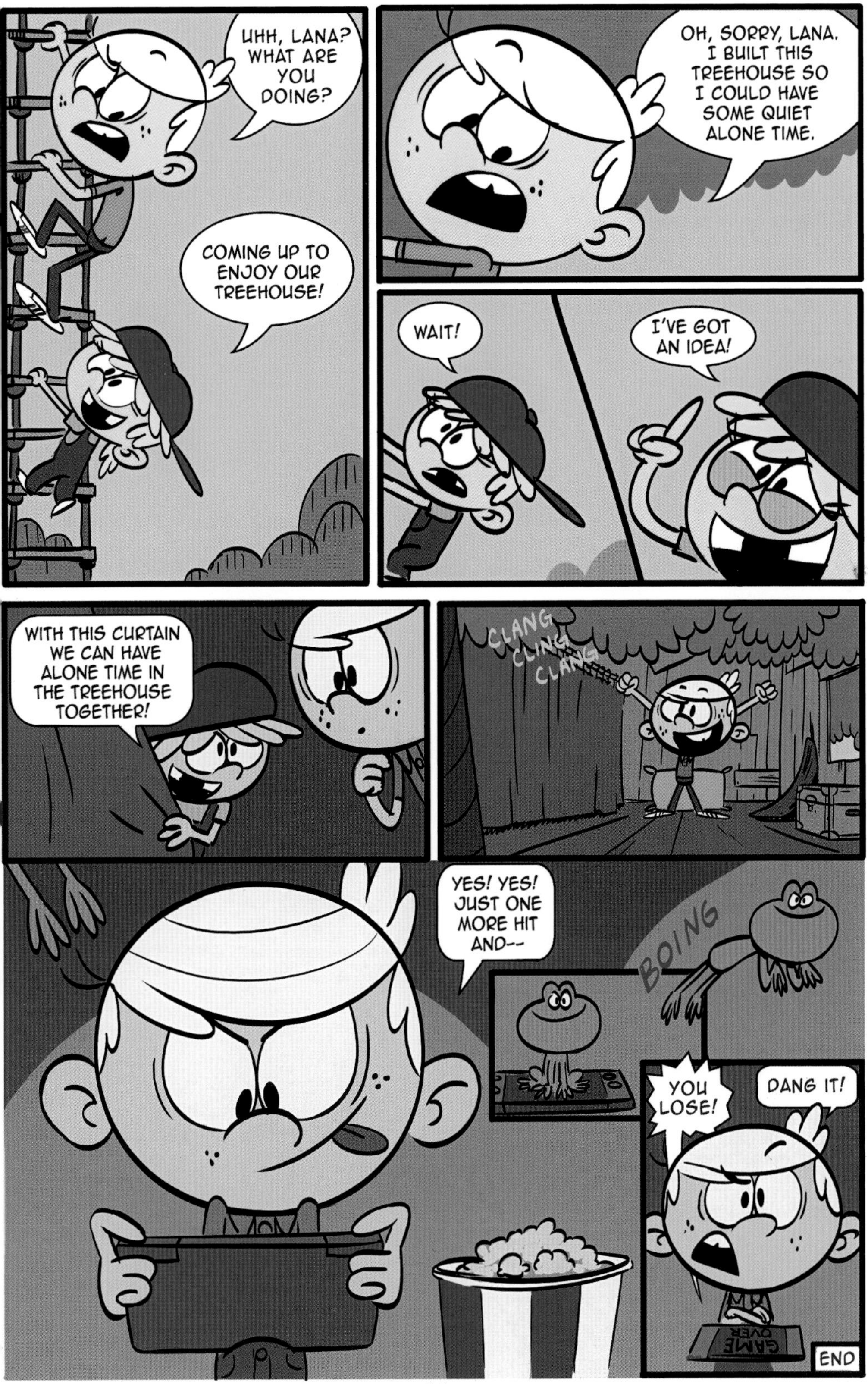

UHH, LANA? WHAT ARE YOU DOING?
COMING UP TO ENJOY OUR TREEHOUSE!
OH, SORRY, LANA. I BUILT THIS TREEHOUSE SO I COULD HAVE SOME QUIET ALONE TIME.
WAIT!
I'VE GOT AN IDEA!
WITH THIS CURTAIN WE CAN HAVE ALONE TIME IN THE TREEHOUSE TOGETHER!
CLANG
CLING
CLANG
YES! YES! JUST ONE MORE HIT AND--
BOING
YOU LOSE!
DANG IT!
GAME OVER
END

"HAI-POO"

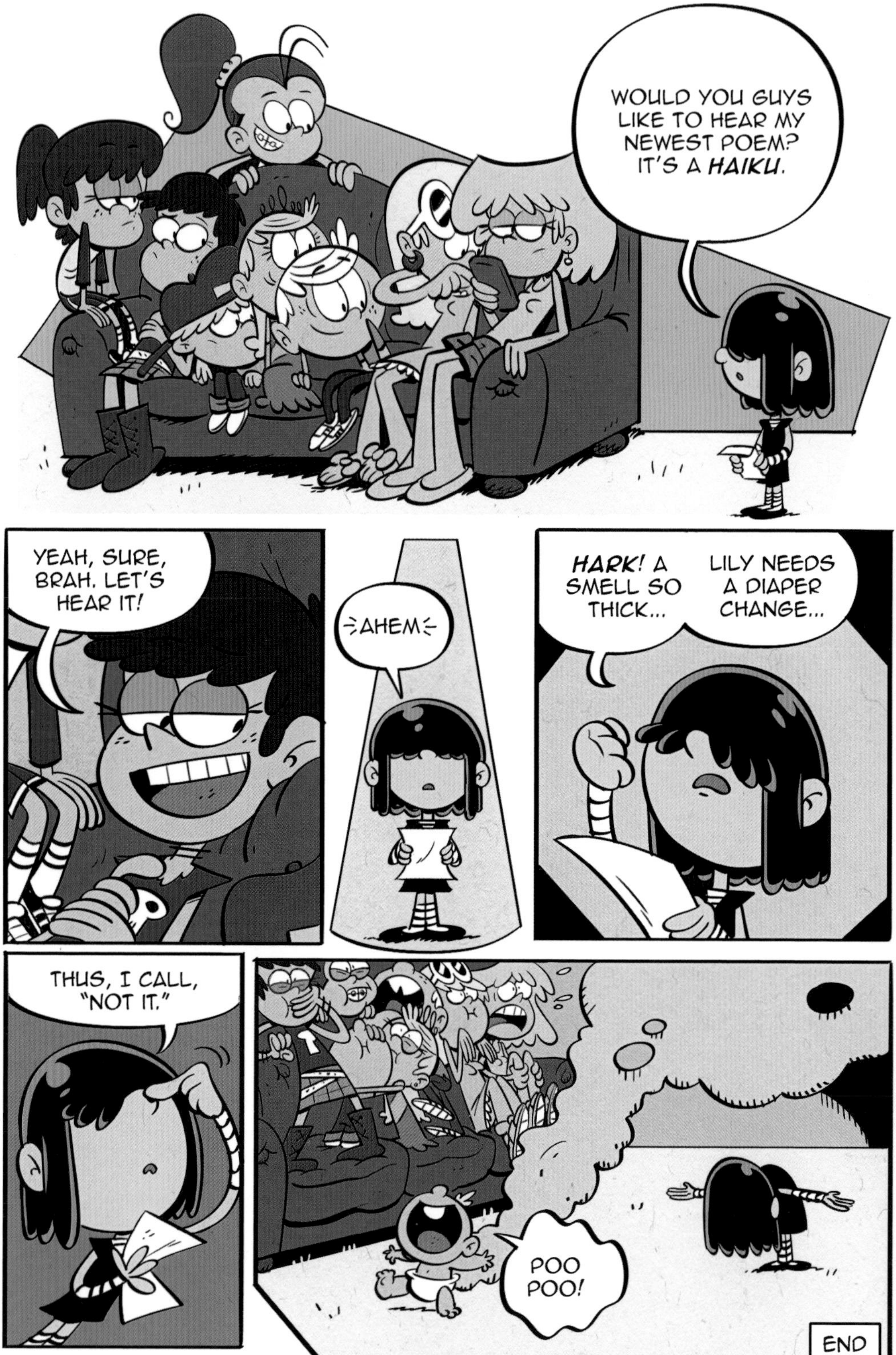
WOULD YOU GUYS LIKE TO HEAR MY NEWEST POEM? IT'S A *HAIKU*.
YEAH, SURE, BRAH. LET'S HEAR IT!
AHEM
HARK! A SMELL SO THICK...
LILY NEEDS A DIAPER CHANGE...
THUS, I CALL, "NOT IT."
POO POO!
END

"STARVING"

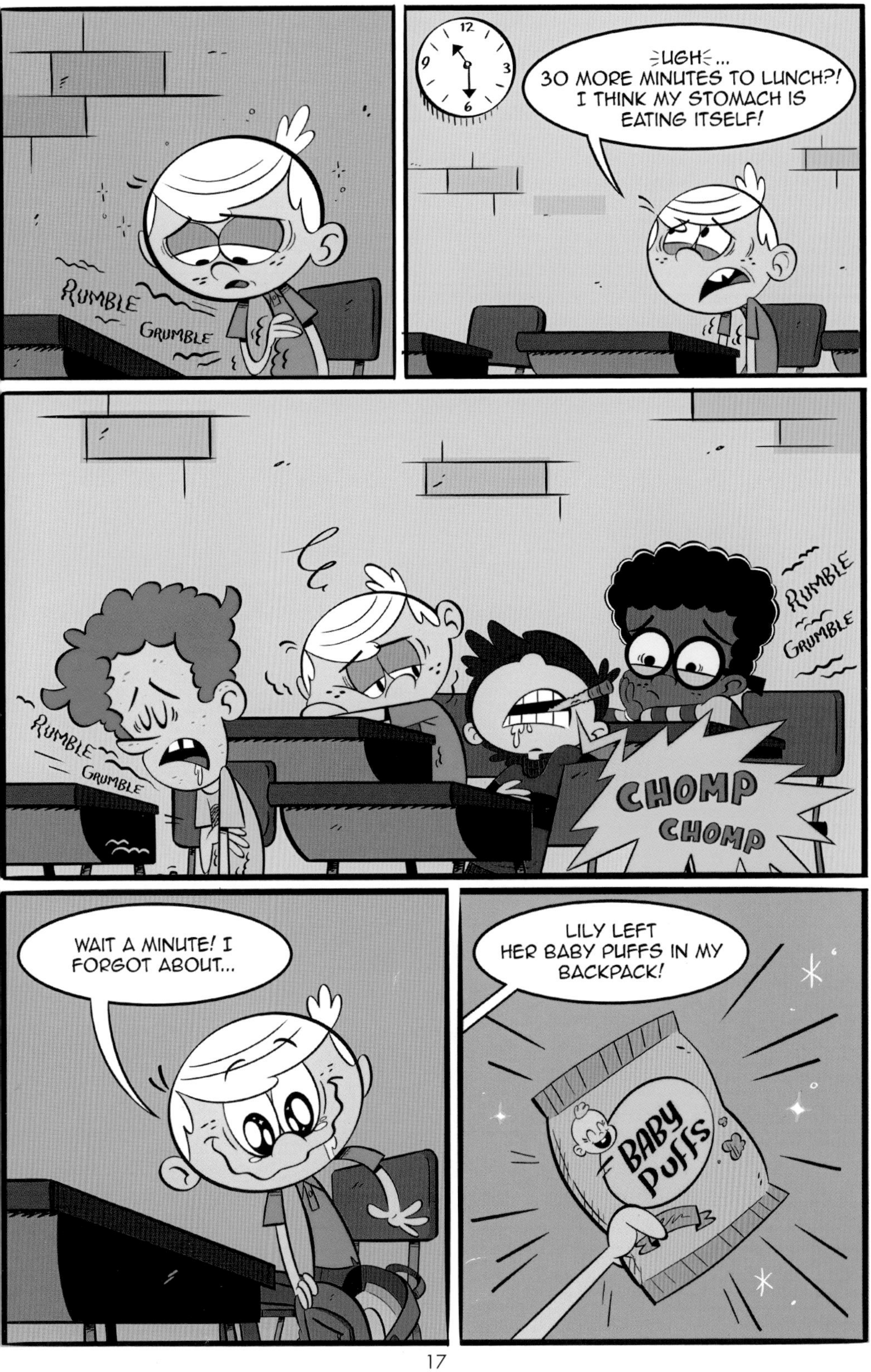
RUMBLE
GRUMBLE
UGH...
30 MORE MINUTES TO LUNCH?! I THINK MY STOMACH IS EATING ITSELF!
RUMBLE
GRUMBLE
RUMBLE
GRUMBLE
CHOMP
CHOMP
WAIT A MINUTE! I FORGOT ABOUT...
LILY LEFT HER BABY PUFFS IN MY BACKPACK!
BABY PUFFS

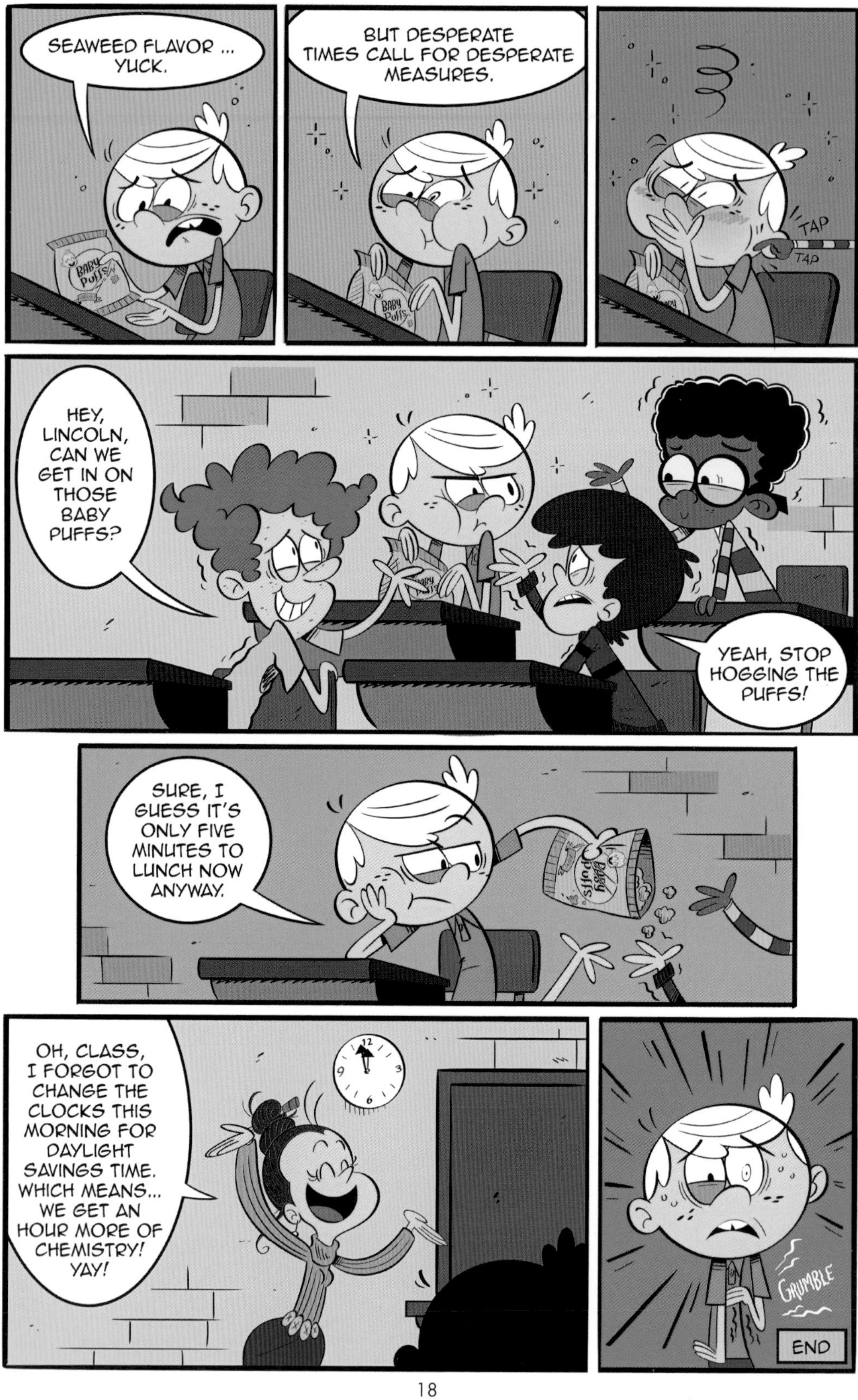
SEAWEED FLAVOR ... YUCK.
BUT DESPERATE TIMES CALL FOR DESPERATE MEASURES.
TAP
TAP
HEY, LINCOLN, CAN WE GET IN ON THOSE BABY PUFFS?
YEAH, STOP HOGGING THE PUFFS!
SURE, I GUESS IT'S ONLY FIVE MINUTES TO LUNCH NOW ANYWAY.
OH, CLASS, I FORGOT TO CHANGE THE CLOCKS THIS MORNING FOR DAYLIGHT SAVINGS TIME. WHICH MEANS... WE GET AN HOUR MORE OF CHEMISTRY! YAY!
GRUMBLE
END

"COOKING WITH THE CASAGRANDES"

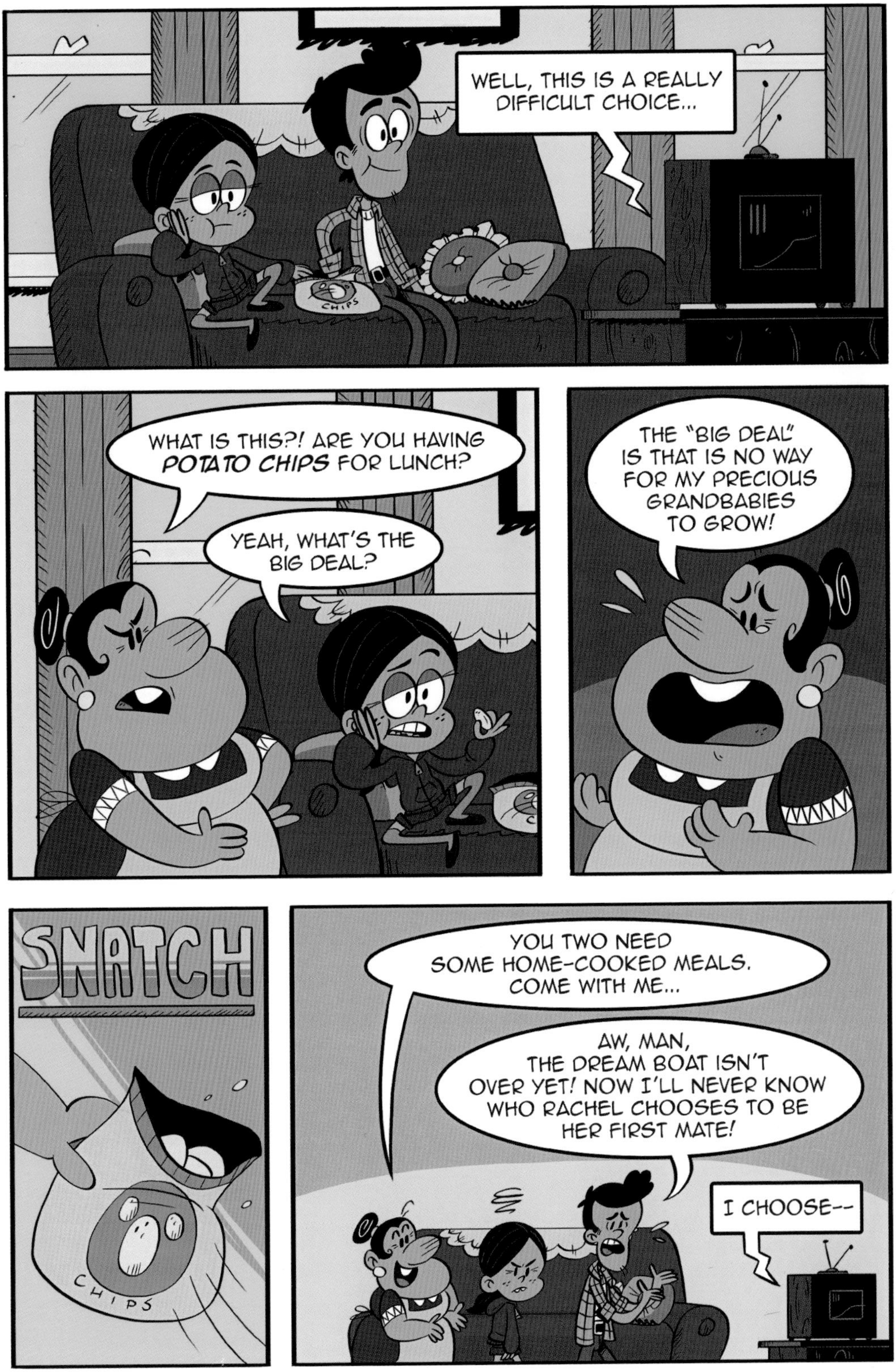

WELL, THIS IS A REALLY DIFFICULT CHOICE...
CHIPS
WHAT IS THIS?! ARE YOU HAVING *POTATO CHIPS* FOR LUNCH?
YEAH, WHAT'S THE BIG DEAL?
THE "BIG DEAL" IS THAT IS NO WAY FOR MY PRECIOUS GRANDBABIES TO GROW!
SNATCH
CHIPS
YOU TWO NEED SOME HOME-COOKED MEALS. COME WITH ME...
AW, MAN, THE DREAM BOAT ISN'T OVER YET! NOW I'LL NEVER KNOW WHO RACHEL CHOOSES TO BE HER FIRST MATE!
I CHOOSE--

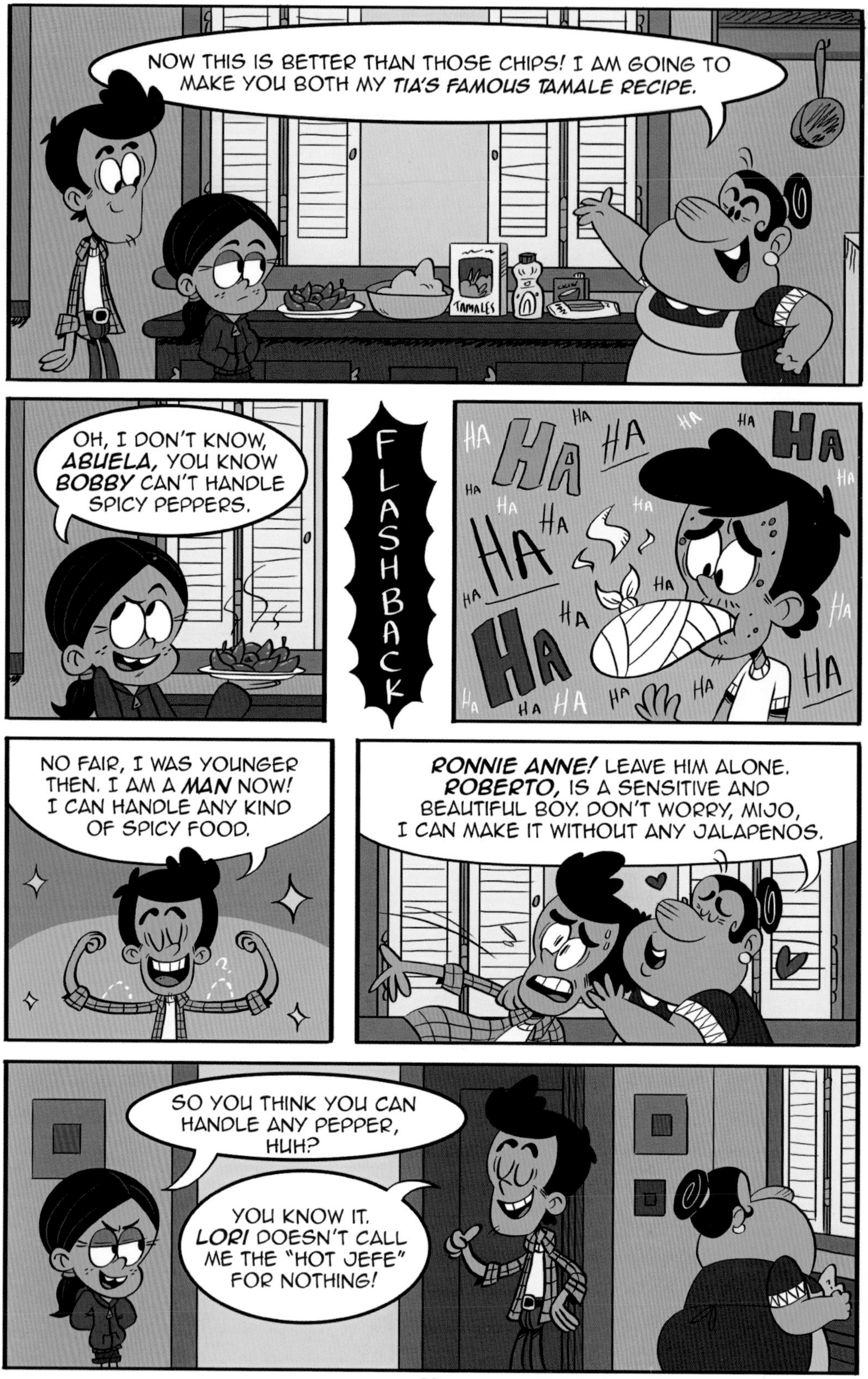
NOW THIS IS BETTER THAN THOSE CHIPS! I AM GOING TO MAKE YOU BOTH MY *TIA'S FAMOUS TAMALE RECIPE.*
TAMALES
OH, I DON'T KNOW, *ABUELA,* YOU KNOW *BOBBY* CAN'T HANDLE SPICY PEPPERS.
FLASHBACK
HA HA HA HA HA HA HA HA HA HA HA HA HA HA HA HA HA HA HA HA HA HA
NO FAIR, I WAS YOUNGER THEN. I AM A *MAN* NOW! I CAN HANDLE ANY KIND OF SPICY FOOD.
RONNIE ANNE! LEAVE HIM ALONE. *ROBERTO,* IS A SENSITIVE AND BEAUTIFUL BOY. DON'T WORRY, MIJO, I CAN MAKE IT WITHOUT ANY JALAPENOS.
SO YOU THINK YOU CAN HANDLE ANY PEPPER, HUH?
YOU KNOW IT. *LORI* DOESN'T CALL ME THE "HOT JEFE" FOR NOTHING!

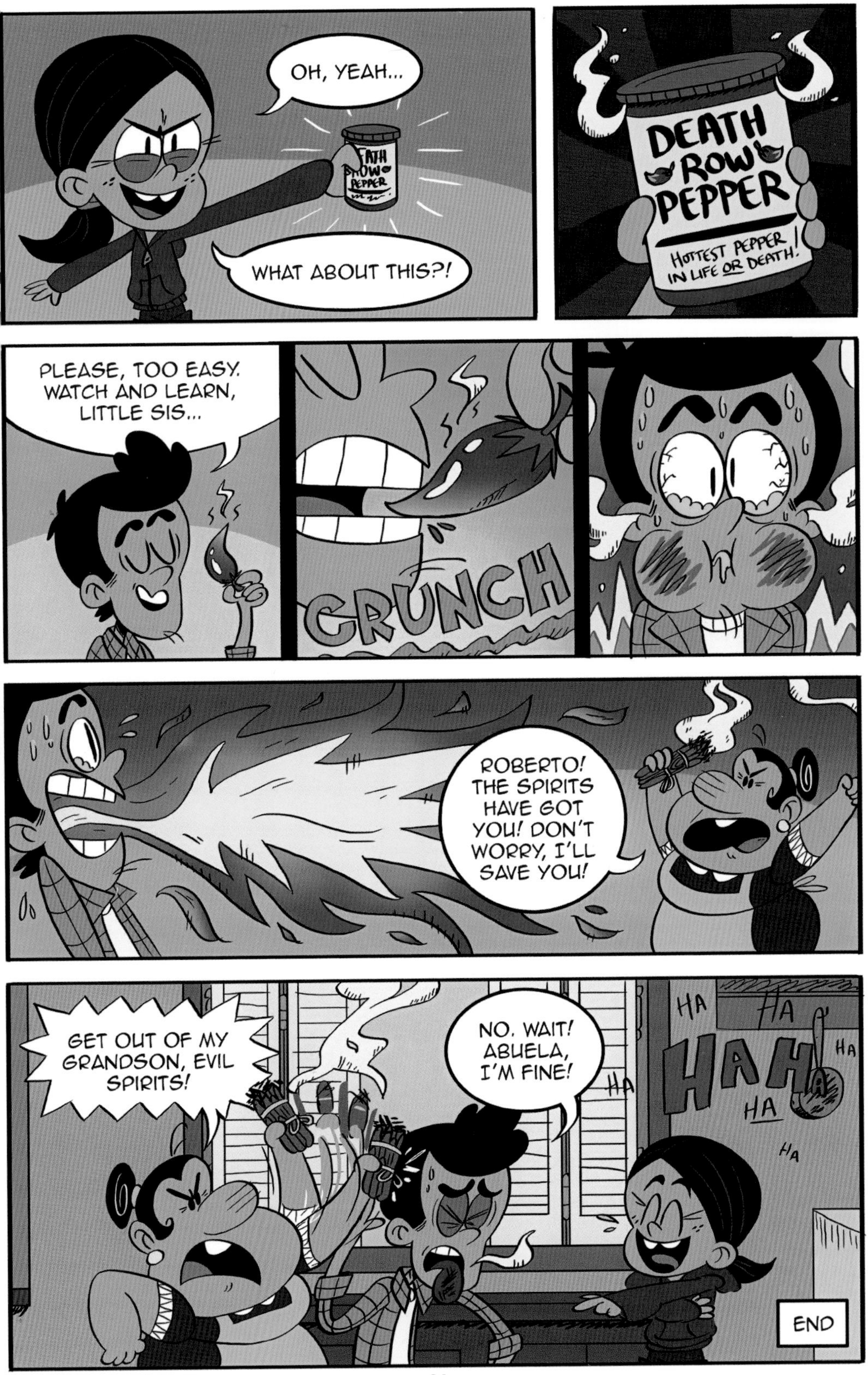
OH, YEAH...
WHAT ABOUT THIS?!
DEATH ROW PEPPER
HOTTEST PEPPER IN LIFE OR DEATH!
PLEASE, TOO EASY. WATCH AND LEARN, LITTLE SIS...
CRUNCH
ROBERTO! THE SPIRITS HAVE GOT YOU! DON'T WORRY, I'LL SAVE YOU!
GET OUT OF MY GRANDSON, EVIL SPIRITS!
NO. WAIT! ABUELA, I'M FINE!
HA HA HAH HA HA HA HA
END

"CODE CRISIS"

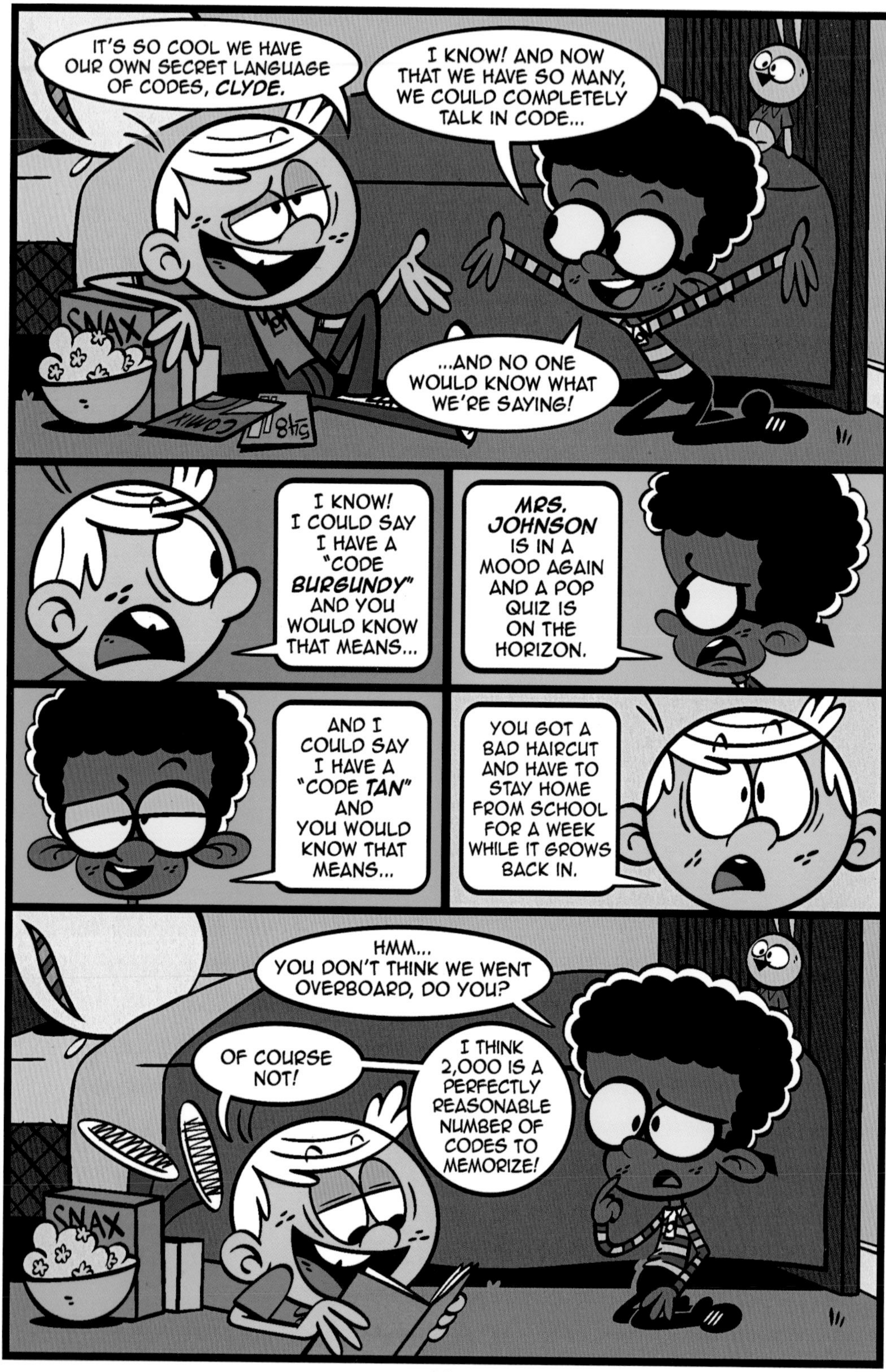
IT'S SO COOL WE HAVE OUR OWN SECRET LANGUAGE OF CODES, *CLYDE.*
I KNOW! AND NOW THAT WE HAVE SO MANY, WE COULD COMPLETELY TALK IN CODE...
...AND NO ONE WOULD KNOW WHAT WE'RE SAYING!
SNAX
COMIX
I KNOW! I COULD SAY I HAVE A "CODE *BURGUNDY*" AND YOU WOULD KNOW THAT MEANS...
MRS. JOHNSON IS IN A MOOD AGAIN AND A POP QUIZ IS ON THE HORIZON.
AND I COULD SAY I HAVE A "CODE *TAN*" AND YOU WOULD KNOW THAT MEANS...
YOU GOT A BAD HAIRCUT AND HAVE TO STAY HOME FROM SCHOOL FOR A WEEK WHILE IT GROWS BACK IN.
HMM... YOU DON'T THINK WE WENT OVERBOARD, DO YOU?
OF COURSE NOT!
I THINK 2,000 IS A PERFECTLY REASONABLE NUMBER OF CODES TO MEMORIZE!
SNAX

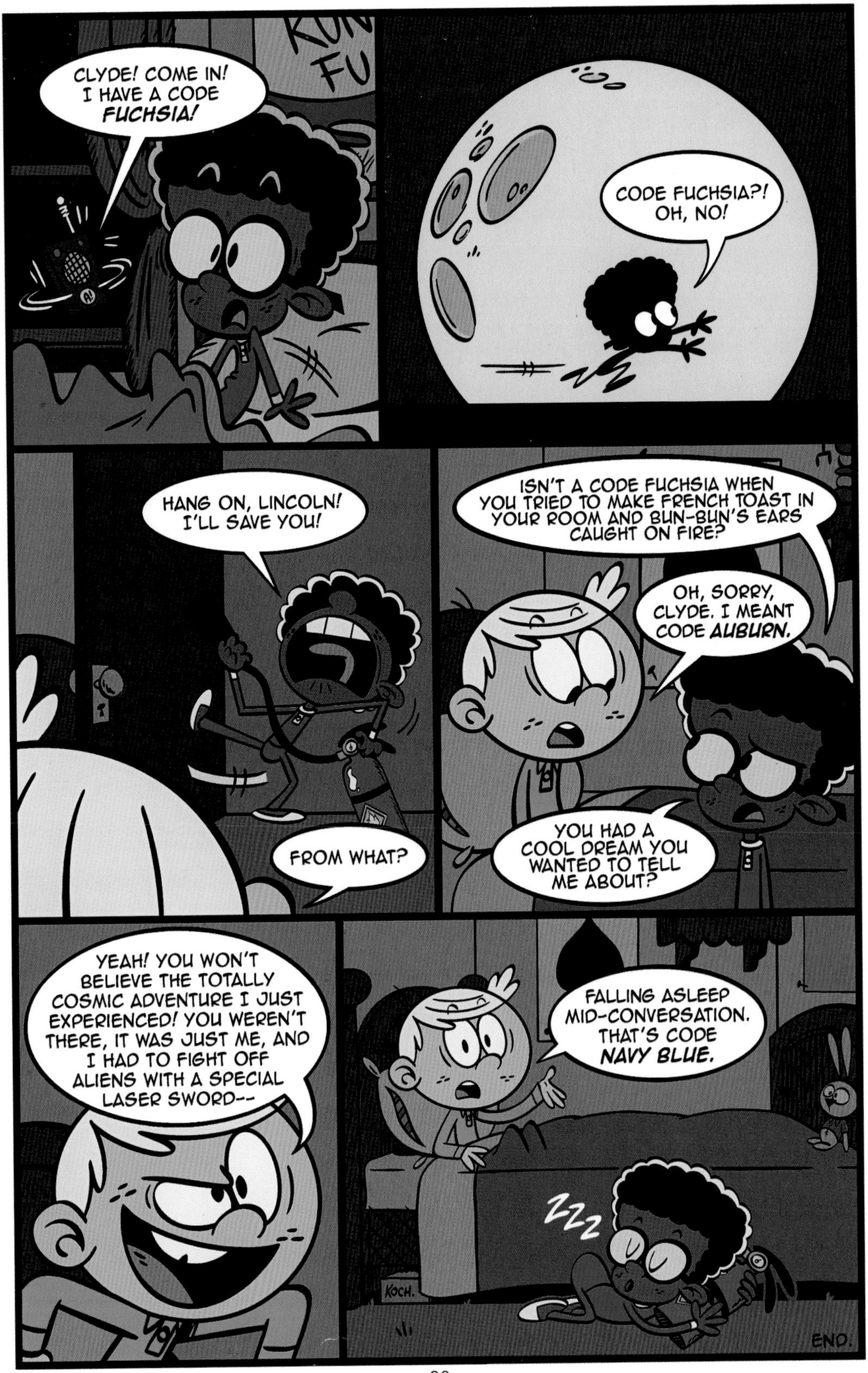
CLYDE! COME IN! I HAVE A CODE FUCHSIA!
CODE FUCHSIA?! OH, NO!
HANG ON, LINCOLN! I'LL SAVE YOU!
FROM WHAT?
ISN'T A CODE FUCHSIA WHEN YOU TRIED TO MAKE FRENCH TOAST IN YOUR ROOM AND BUN-BUN'S EARS CAUGHT ON FIRE?
OH, SORRY, CLYDE. I MEANT CODE AUBURN.
YOU HAD A COOL DREAM YOU WANTED TO TELL ME ABOUT?
YEAH! YOU WON'T BELIEVE THE TOTALLY COSMIC ADVENTURE I JUST EXPERIENCED! YOU WEREN'T THERE, IT WAS JUST ME, AND I HAD TO FIGHT OFF ALIENS WITH A SPECIAL LASER SWORD--
FALLING ASLEEP MID-CONVERSATION. THAT'S CODE NAVY BLUE.
ZZZ
KOCH.
END.

"DISJOINT CUSTODY"

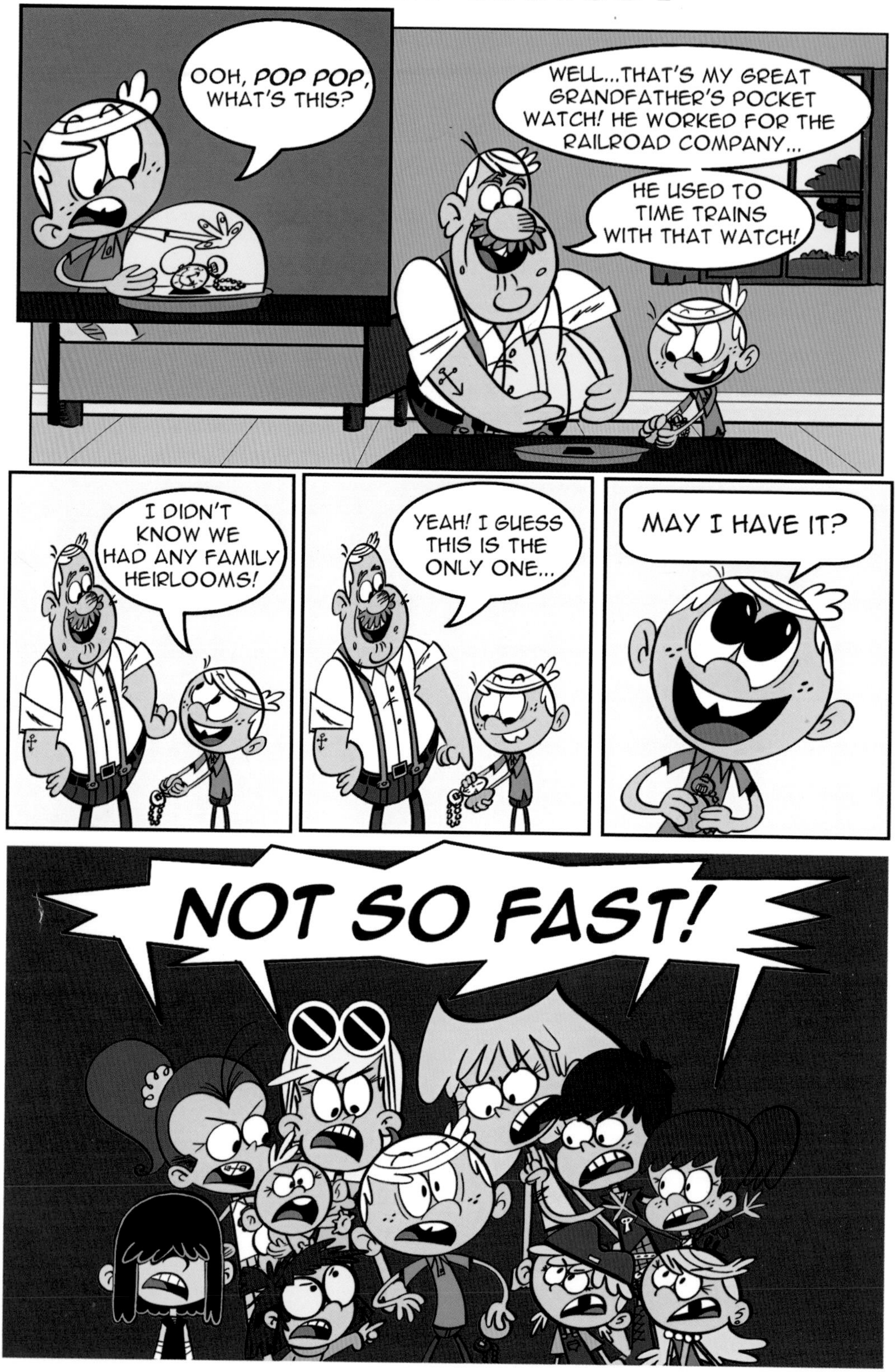
OOH, *POP POP*, WHAT'S THIS?
WELL...THAT'S MY GREAT GRANDFATHER'S POCKET WATCH! HE WORKED FOR THE RAILROAD COMPANY...
HE USED TO TIME TRAINS WITH THAT WATCH!
I DIDN'T KNOW WE HAD ANY FAMILY HEIRLOOMS!
YEAH! I GUESS THIS IS THE ONLY ONE...
MAY I HAVE IT?
NOT SO FAST!

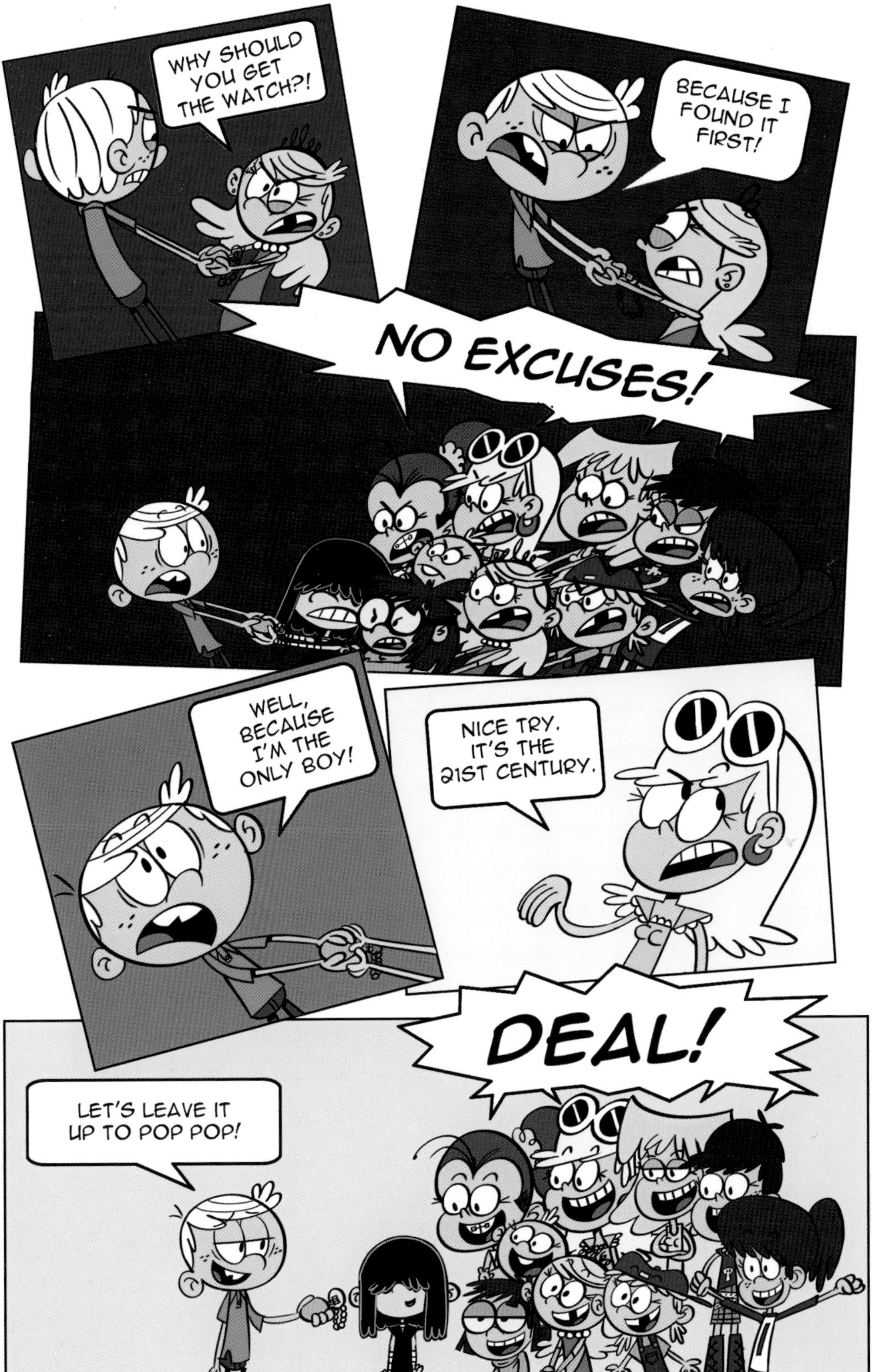
WHY SHOULD YOU GET THE WATCH?!
BECAUSE I FOUND IT FIRST!
NO EXCUSES!
WELL, BECAUSE I'M THE ONLY BOY!
NICE TRY. IT'S THE 21ST CENTURY.
LET'S LEAVE IT UP TO POP POP!
DEAL!

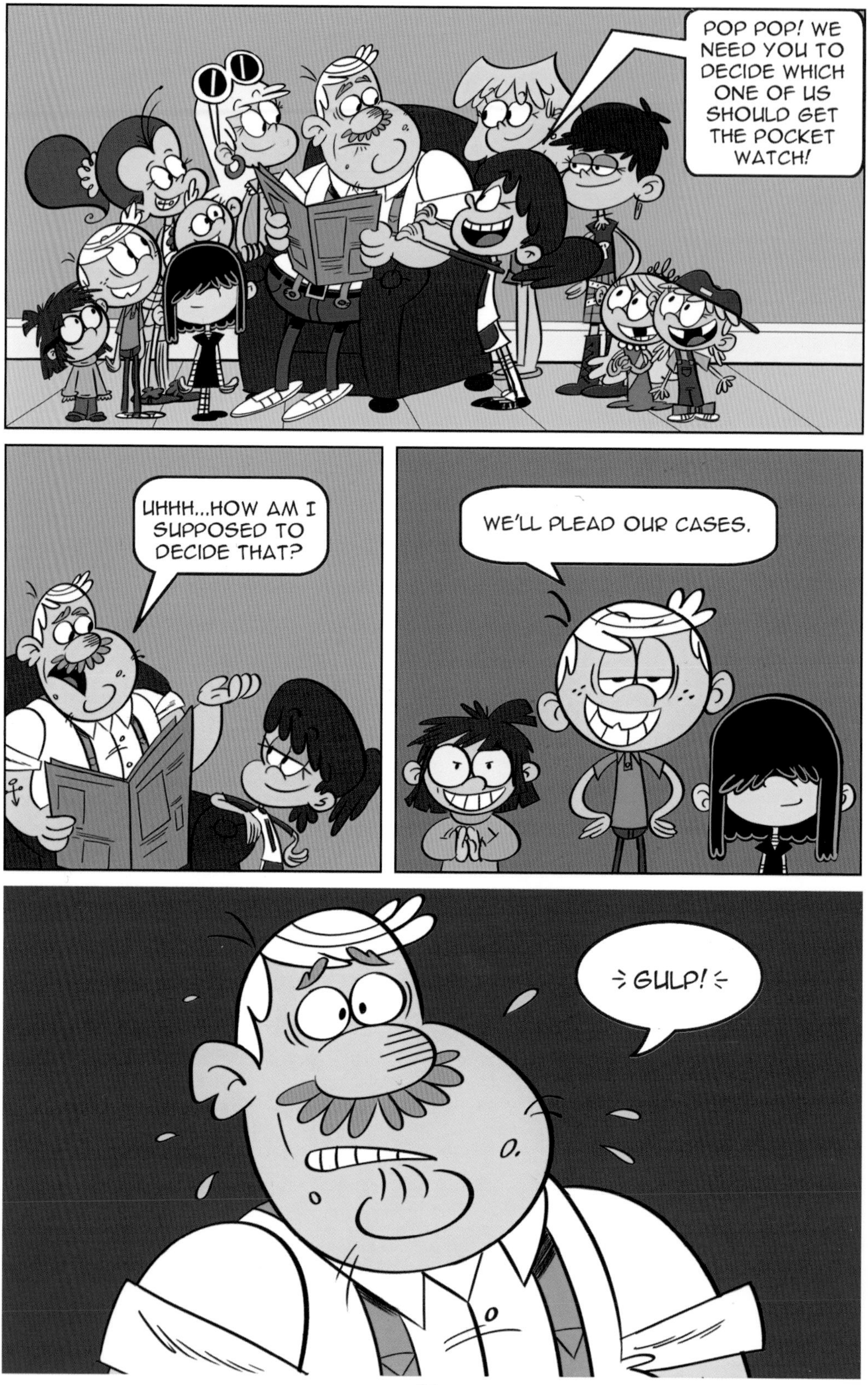
POP POP! WE NEED YOU TO DECIDE WHICH ONE OF US SHOULD GET THE POCKET WATCH!
UHHH...HOW AM I SUPPOSED TO DECIDE THAT?
WE'LL PLEAD OUR CASES.
GULP!

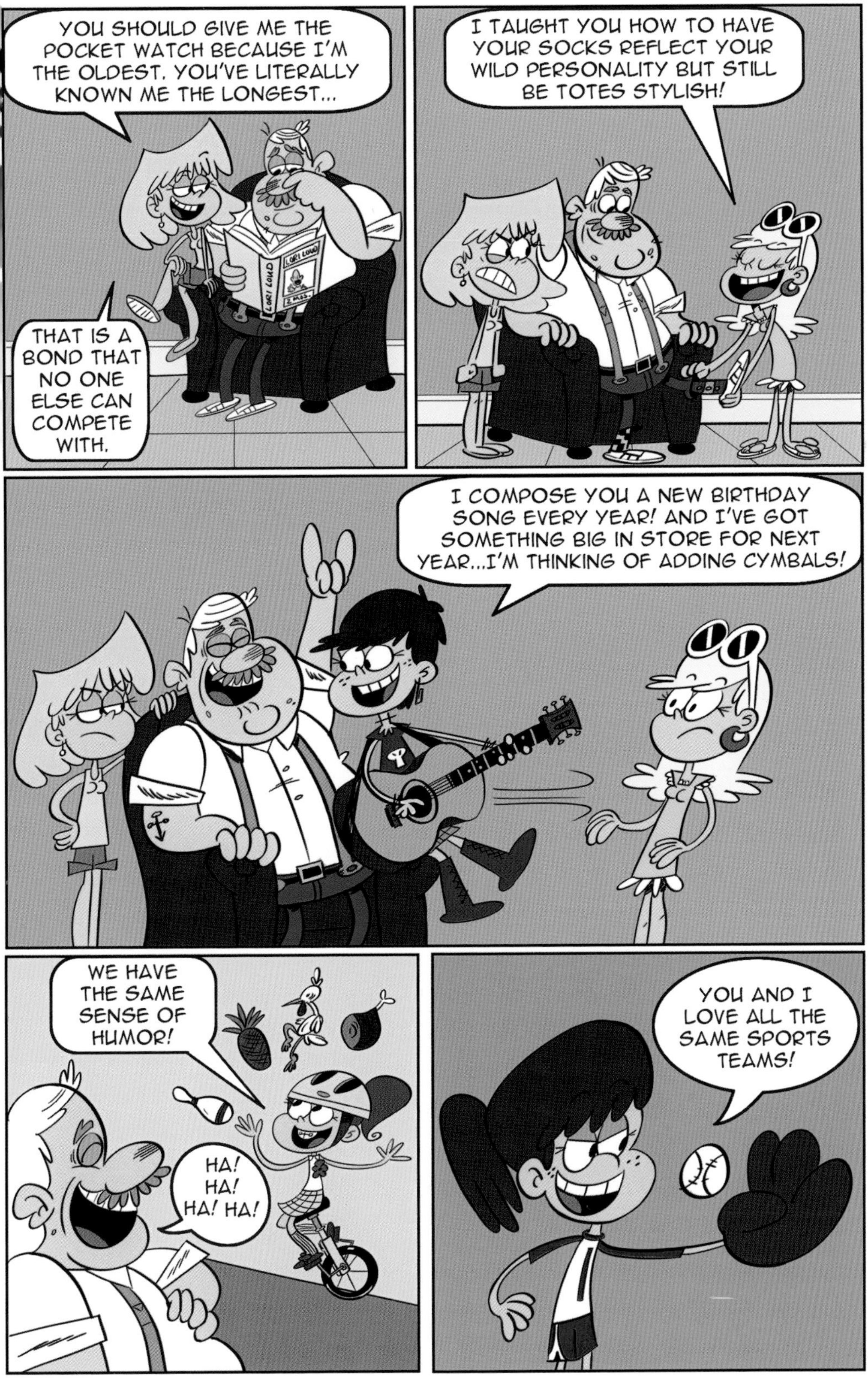
YOU SHOULD GIVE ME THE POCKET WATCH BECAUSE I'M THE OLDEST. YOU'VE LITERALLY KNOWN ME THE LONGEST...
THAT IS A BOND THAT NO ONE ELSE CAN COMPETE WITH.
LORI LOUD
I TAUGHT YOU HOW TO HAVE YOUR SOCKS REFLECT YOUR WILD PERSONALITY BUT STILL BE TOTES STYLISH!
I COMPOSE YOU A NEW BIRTHDAY SONG EVERY YEAR! AND I'VE GOT SOMETHING BIG IN STORE FOR NEXT YEAR...I'M THINKING OF ADDING CYMBALS!
WE HAVE THE SAME SENSE OF HUMOR!
HA! HA! HA! HA!
YOU AND I LOVE ALL THE SAME SPORTS TEAMS!

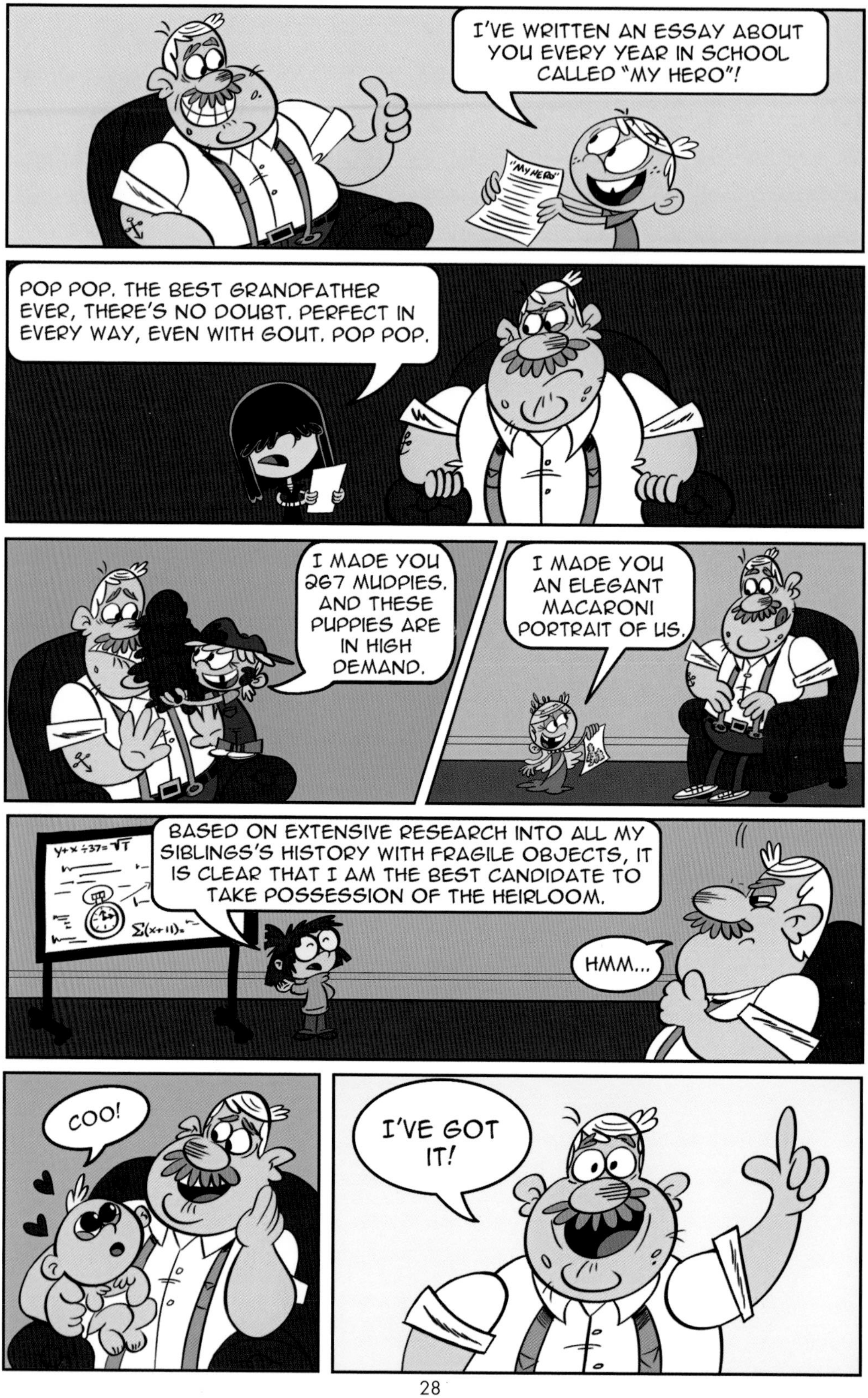
I'VE WRITTEN AN ESSAY ABOUT YOU EVERY YEAR IN SCHOOL CALLED "MY HERO"!
"MY HERO"
POP POP. THE BEST GRANDFATHER EVER, THERE'S NO DOUBT. PERFECT IN EVERY WAY, EVEN WITH GOUT. POP POP.
I MADE YOU 267 MUDPIES. AND THESE PUPPIES ARE IN HIGH DEMAND.
I MADE YOU AN ELEGANT MACARONI PORTRAIT OF US.
BASED ON EXTENSIVE RESEARCH INTO ALL MY SIBLINGS'S HISTORY WITH FRAGILE OBJECTS, IT IS CLEAR THAT I AM THE BEST CANDIDATE TO TAKE POSSESSION OF THE HEIRLOOM.
HMM...
COO!
I'VE GOT IT!

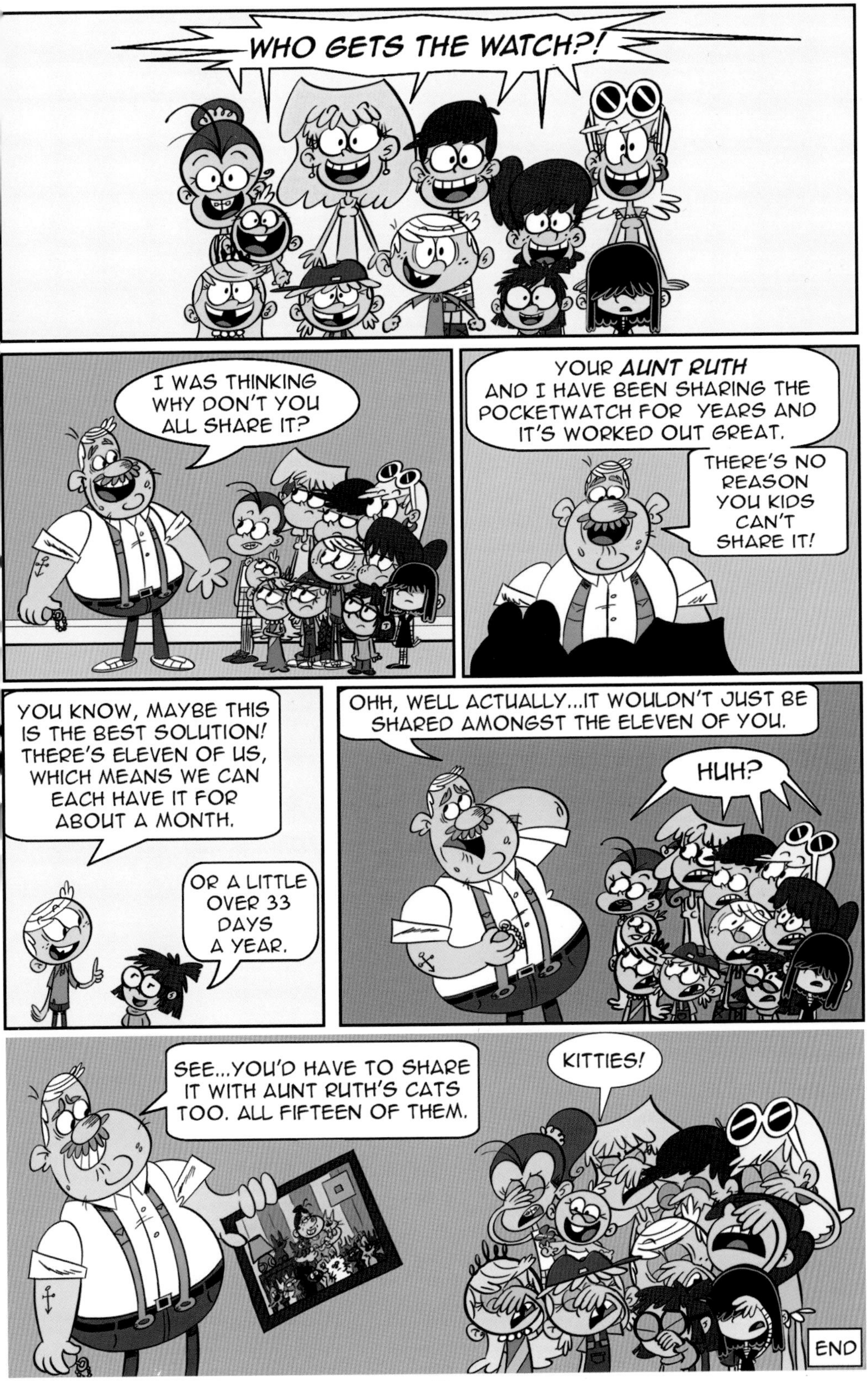
WHO GETS THE WATCH?!
I WAS THINKING WHY DON'T YOU ALL SHARE IT?
YOUR AUNT RUTH AND I HAVE BEEN SHARING THE POCKETWATCH FOR YEARS AND IT'S WORKED OUT GREAT.
THERE'S NO REASON YOU KIDS CAN'T SHARE IT!
YOU KNOW, MAYBE THIS IS THE BEST SOLUTION! THERE'S ELEVEN OF US, WHICH MEANS WE CAN EACH HAVE IT FOR ABOUT A MONTH.
OR A LITTLE OVER 33 DAYS A YEAR.
OHH, WELL ACTUALLY...IT WOULDN'T JUST BE SHARED AMONGST THE ELEVEN OF YOU.
HUH?
SEE...YOU'D HAVE TO SHARE IT WITH AUNT RUTH'S CATS TOO. ALL FIFTEEN OF THEM.
KITTIES!
END

"THE LOUD JOURNEY"

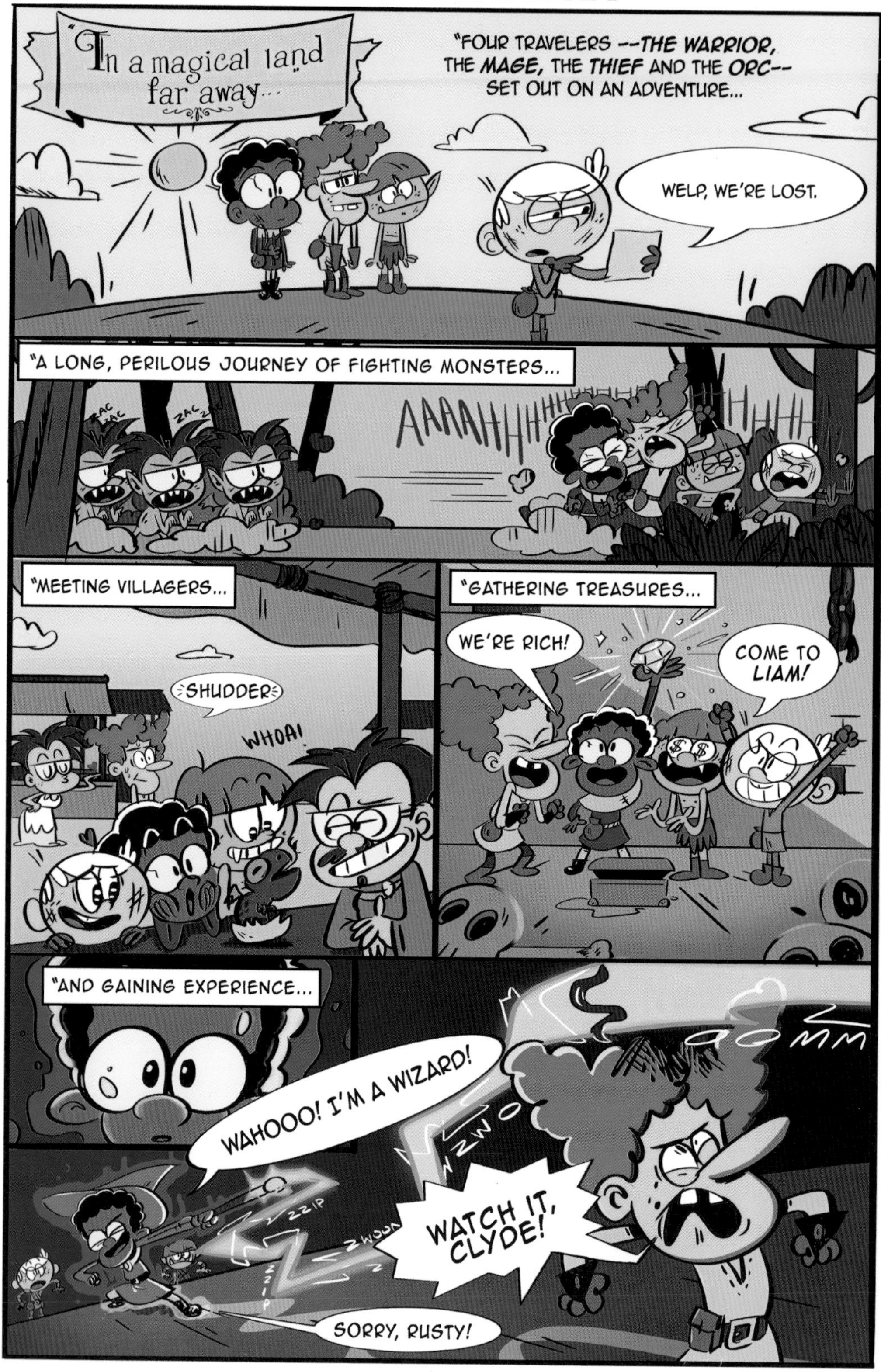

"In a magical land far away...
"FOUR TRAVELERS --THE WARRIOR, THE MAGE, THE THIEF AND THE ORC-- SET OUT ON AN ADVENTURE...
WELP, WE'RE LOST.
"A LONG, PERILOUS JOURNEY OF FIGHTING MONSTERS...
AAAAHHHHHHHH
"MEETING VILLAGERS...
SHUDDER
WHOA!
"GATHERING TREASURES...
WE'RE RICH!
COME TO LIAM!
"AND GAINING EXPERIENCE...
WAHOOO! I'M A WIZARD!
WATCH IT, CLYDE!
SORRY, RUSTY!

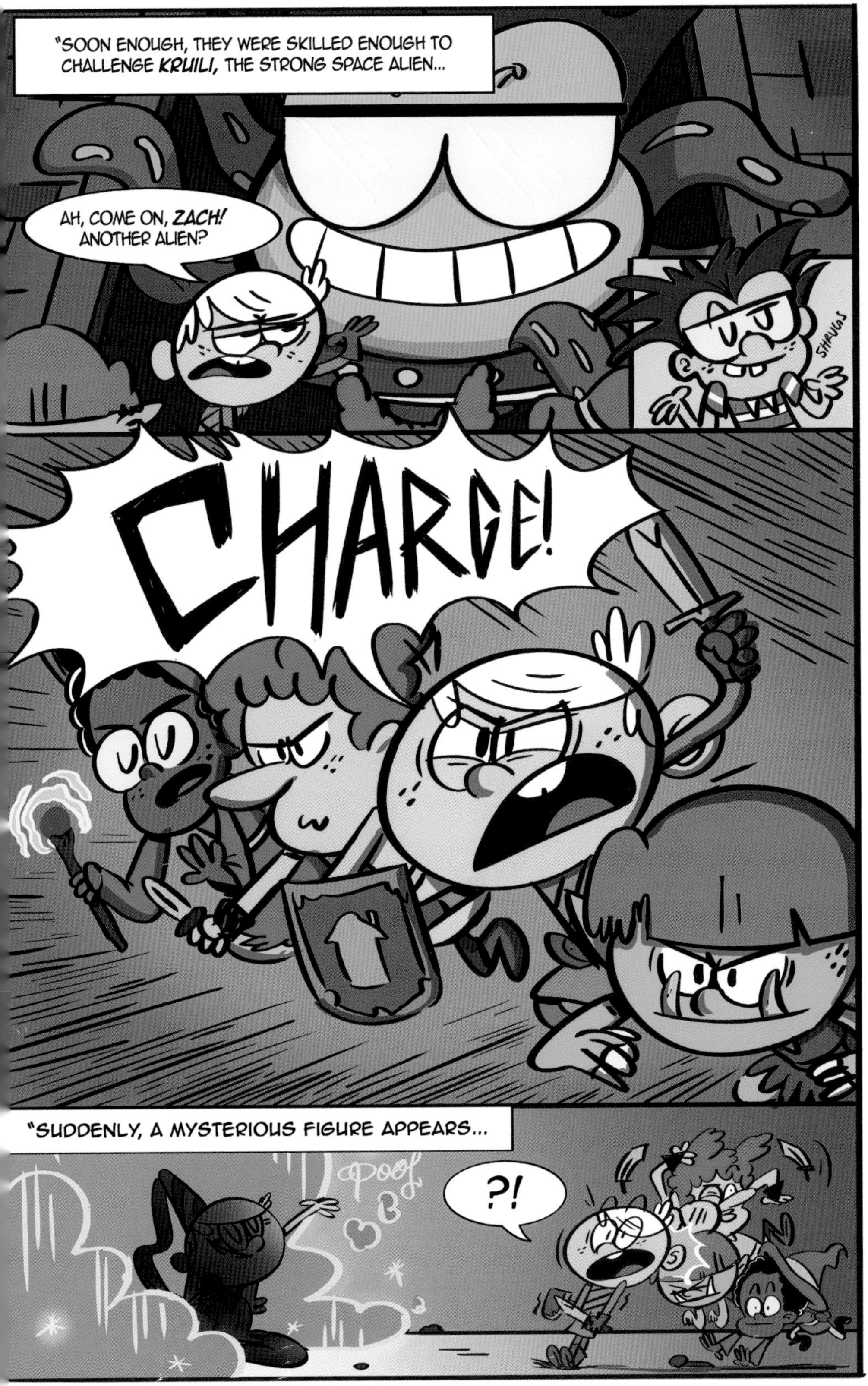
"SOON ENOUGH, THEY WERE SKILLED ENOUGH TO CHALLENGE KRUILI, THE STRONG SPACE ALIEN...
AH, COME ON, ZACH! ANOTHER ALIEN?
SHRUGS
CHARGE!
"SUDDENLY, A MYSTERIOUS FIGURE APPEARS...
POOF
?!

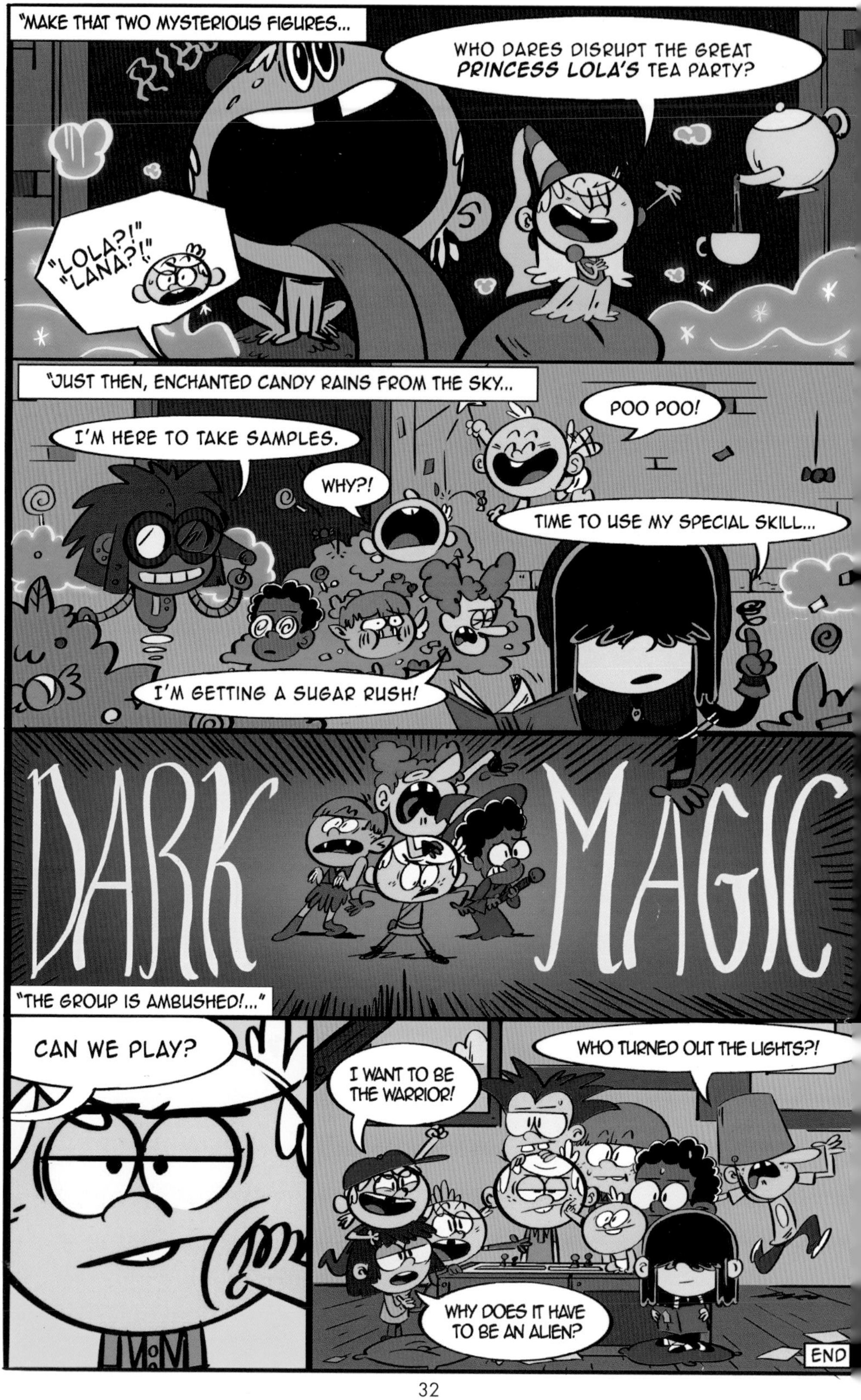
"MAKE THAT TWO MYSTERIOUS FIGURES...
WHO DARES DISRUPT THE GREAT *PRINCESS LOLA'S* TEA PARTY?
"LOLA?!" "LANA?!"
"JUST THEN, ENCHANTED CANDY RAINS FROM THE SKY...
I'M HERE TO TAKE SAMPLES.
WHY?!
POO POO!
TIME TO USE MY SPECIAL SKILL...
I'M GETTING A SUGAR RUSH!
DARK MAGIC
"THE GROUP IS AMBUSHED!..."
CAN WE PLAY?
I WANT TO BE THE WARRIOR!
WHO TURNED OUT THE LIGHTS?!
WHY DOES IT HAVE TO BE AN ALIEN?
END

"WORKED UP"

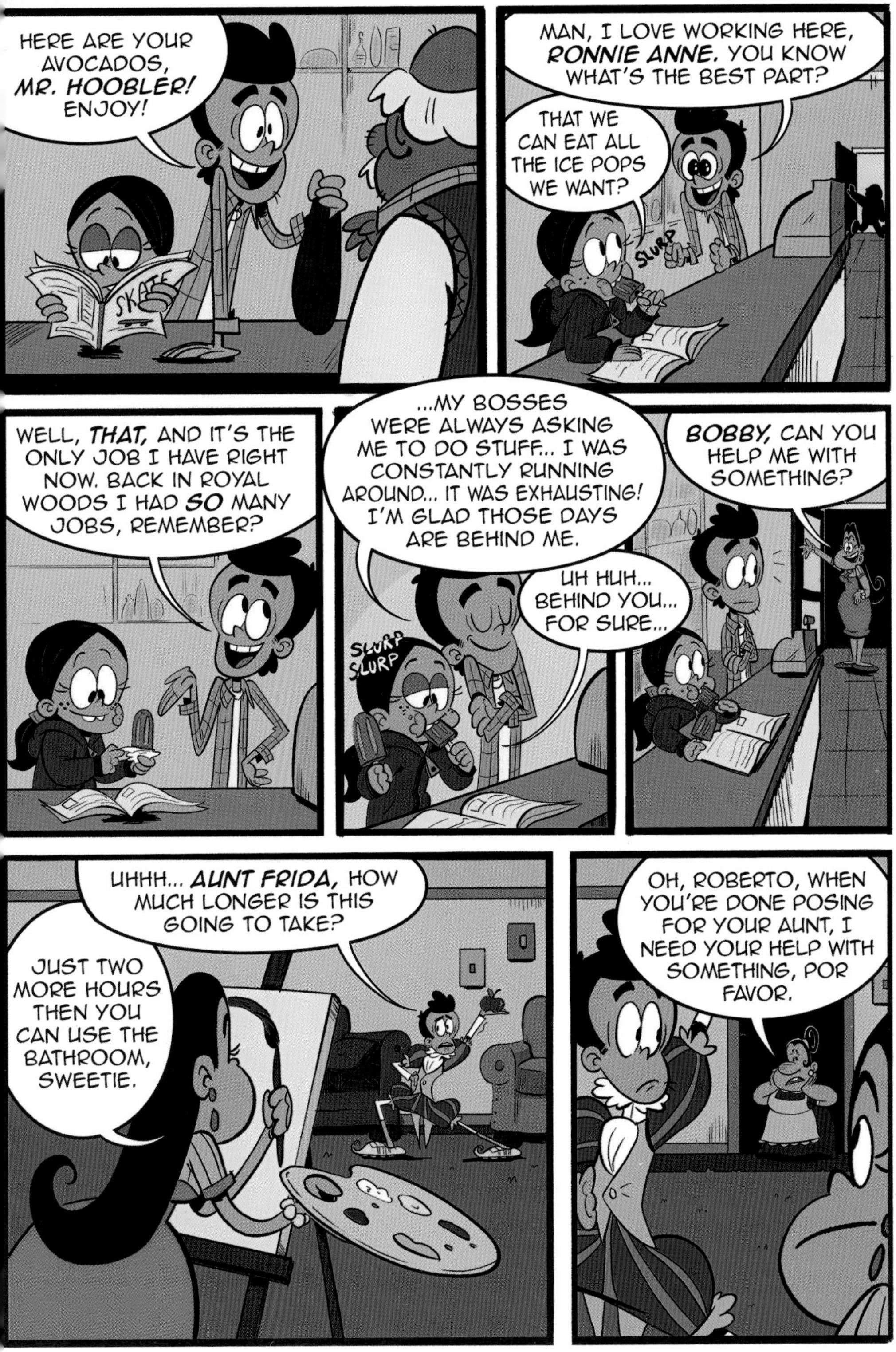
HERE ARE YOUR AVOCADOS, MR. HOOBLER! ENJOY!
SKATE
MAN, I LOVE WORKING HERE, RONNIE ANNE. YOU KNOW WHAT'S THE BEST PART?
THAT WE CAN EAT ALL THE ICE POPS WE WANT?
SLURP
WELL, THAT, AND IT'S THE ONLY JOB I HAVE RIGHT NOW. BACK IN ROYAL WOODS I HAD SO MANY JOBS, REMEMBER?
...MY BOSSES WERE ALWAYS ASKING ME TO DO STUFF... I WAS CONSTANTLY RUNNING AROUND... IT WAS EXHAUSTING! I'M GLAD THOSE DAYS ARE BEHIND ME.
SLURP SLURP
UH HUH... BEHIND YOU... FOR SURE...
BOBBY, CAN YOU HELP ME WITH SOMETHING?
UHHH... AUNT FRIDA, HOW MUCH LONGER IS THIS GOING TO TAKE?
JUST TWO MORE HOURS THEN YOU CAN USE THE BATHROOM, SWEETIE.
OH, ROBERTO, WHEN YOU'RE DONE POSING FOR YOUR AUNT, I NEED YOUR HELP WITH SOMETHING, POR FAVOR.

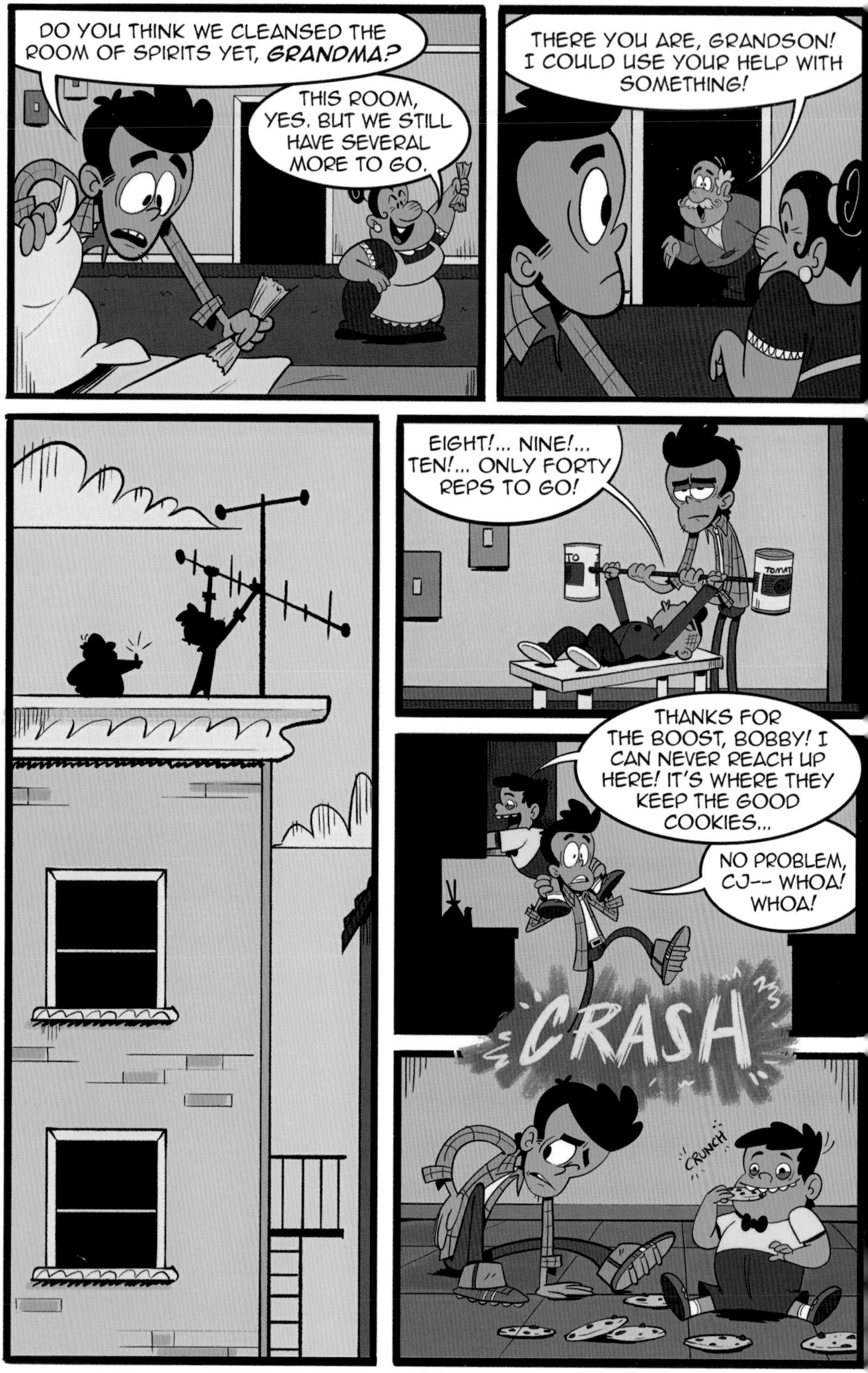
DO YOU THINK WE CLEANSED THE ROOM OF SPIRITS YET, GRANDMA?
THIS ROOM, YES. BUT WE STILL HAVE SEVERAL MORE TO GO.
THERE YOU ARE, GRANDSON! I COULD USE YOUR HELP WITH SOMETHING!
EIGHT!... NINE!... TEN!... ONLY FORTY REPS TO GO!
THANKS FOR THE BOOST, BOBBY! I CAN NEVER REACH UP HERE! IT'S WHERE THEY KEEP THE GOOD COOKIES...
NO PROBLEM, CJ-- WHOA! WHOA!
CRASH
CRUNCH

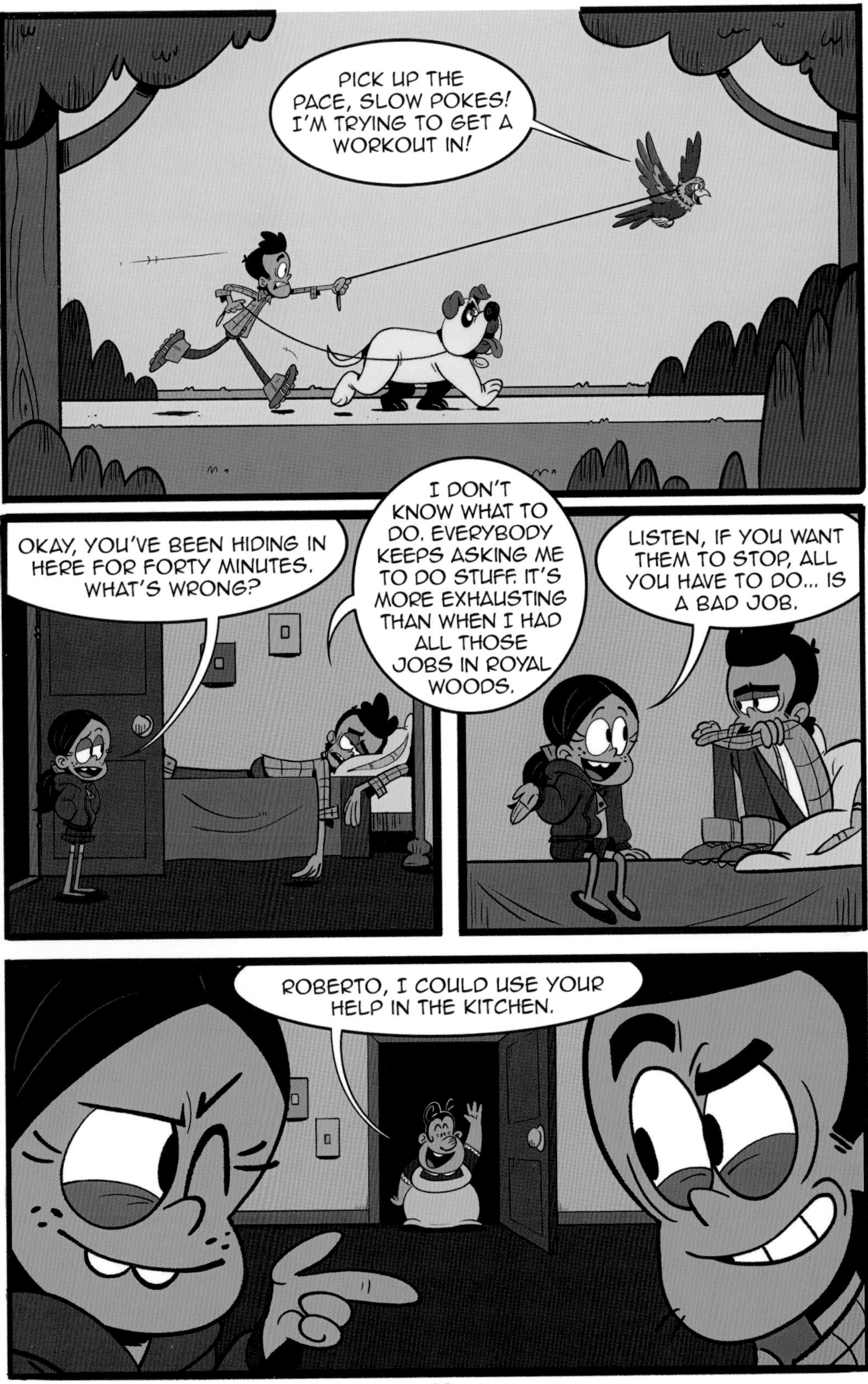
PICK UP THE PACE, SLOW POKES! I'M TRYING TO GET A WORKOUT IN!
OKAY, YOU'VE BEEN HIDING IN HERE FOR FORTY MINUTES. WHAT'S WRONG?
I DON'T KNOW WHAT TO DO. EVERYBODY KEEPS ASKING ME TO DO STUFF. IT'S MORE EXHAUSTING THAN WHEN I HAD ALL THOSE JOBS IN ROYAL WOODS.
LISTEN, IF YOU WANT THEM TO STOP, ALL YOU HAVE TO DO... IS A BAD JOB.
ROBERTO, I COULD USE YOUR HELP IN THE KITCHEN.

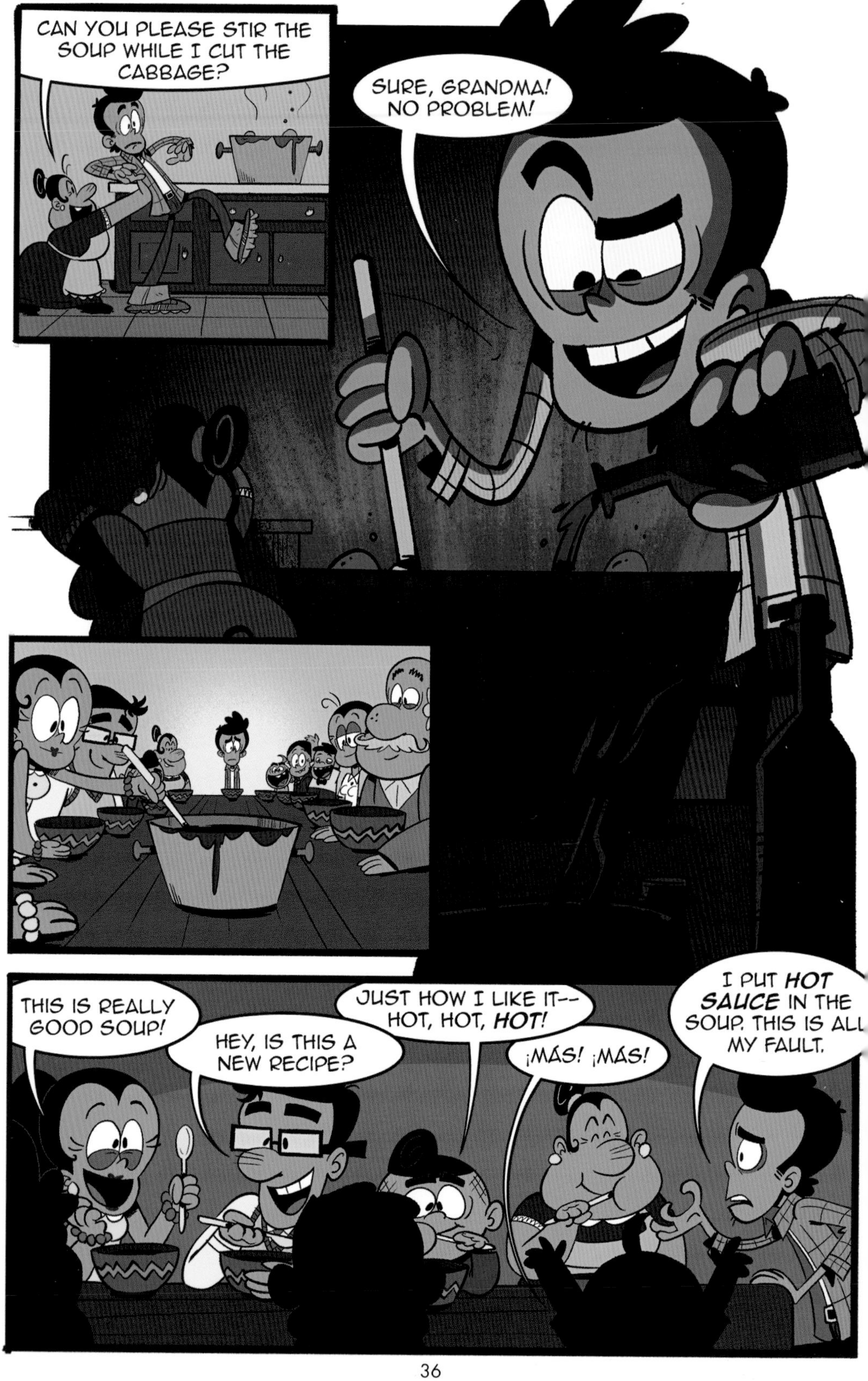
CAN YOU PLEASE STIR THE SOUP WHILE I CUT THE CABBAGE?
SURE, GRANDMA! NO PROBLEM!
THIS IS REALLY GOOD SOUP!
HEY, IS THIS A NEW RECIPE?
JUST HOW I LIKE IT-- HOT, HOT, *HOT*!
¡MÁS! ¡MÁS!
I PUT *HOT SAUCE* IN THE SOUP. THIS IS ALL MY FAULT.

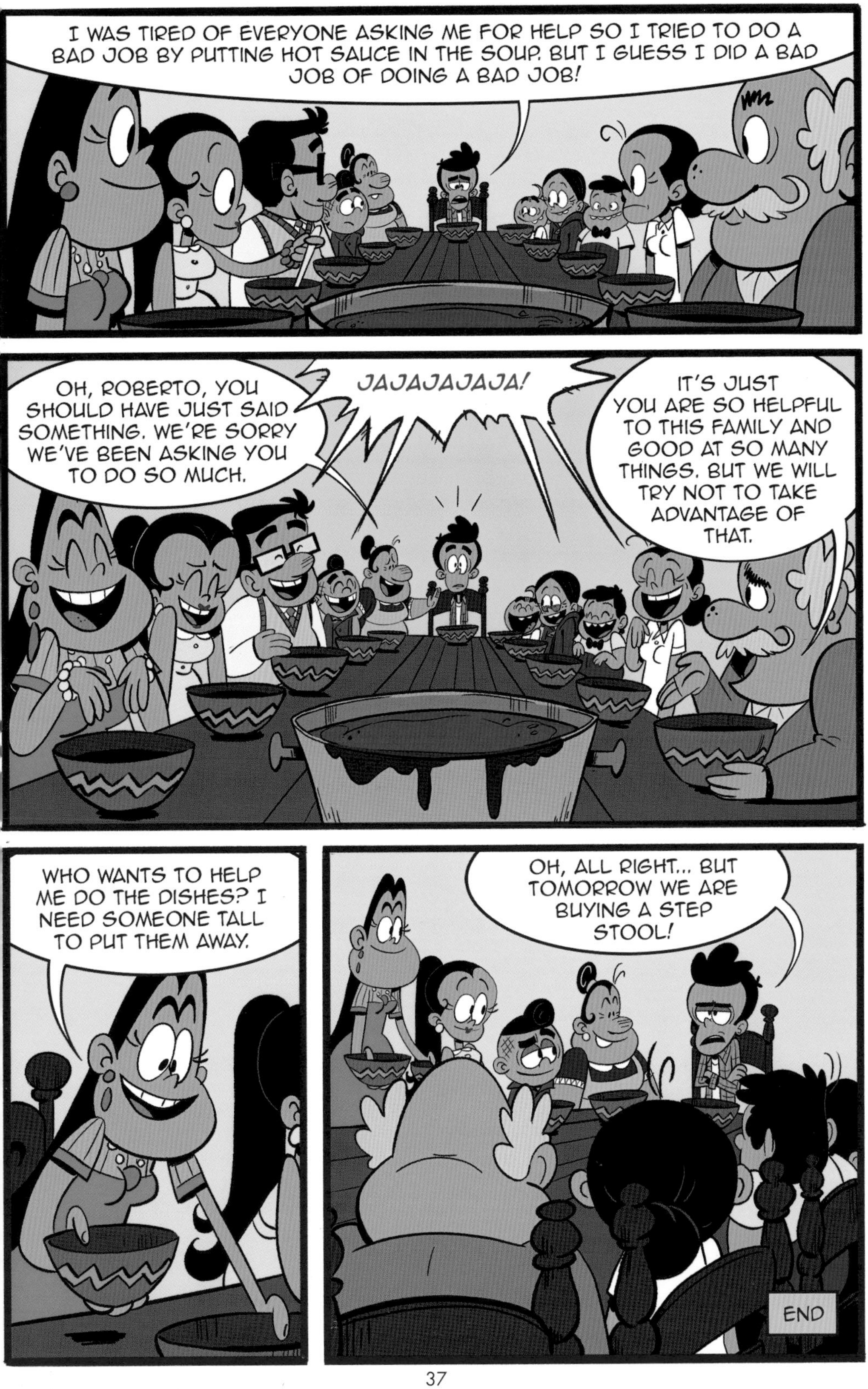
I WAS TIRED OF EVERYONE ASKING ME FOR HELP SO I TRIED TO DO A BAD JOB BY PUTTING HOT SAUCE IN THE SOUP. BUT I GUESS I DID A BAD JOB OF DOING A BAD JOB!
OH, ROBERTO, YOU SHOULD HAVE JUST SAID SOMETHING. WE'RE SORRY WE'VE BEEN ASKING YOU TO DO SO MUCH.
JAJAJAJAJA!
IT'S JUST YOU ARE SO HELPFUL TO THIS FAMILY AND GOOD AT SO MANY THINGS. BUT WE WILL TRY NOT TO TAKE ADVANTAGE OF THAT.
WHO WANTS TO HELP ME DO THE DISHES? I NEED SOMEONE TALL TO PUT THEM AWAY.
OH, ALL RIGHT... BUT TOMORROW WE ARE BUYING A STEP STOOL!
END

"MAYBE IT'S NATURAL"

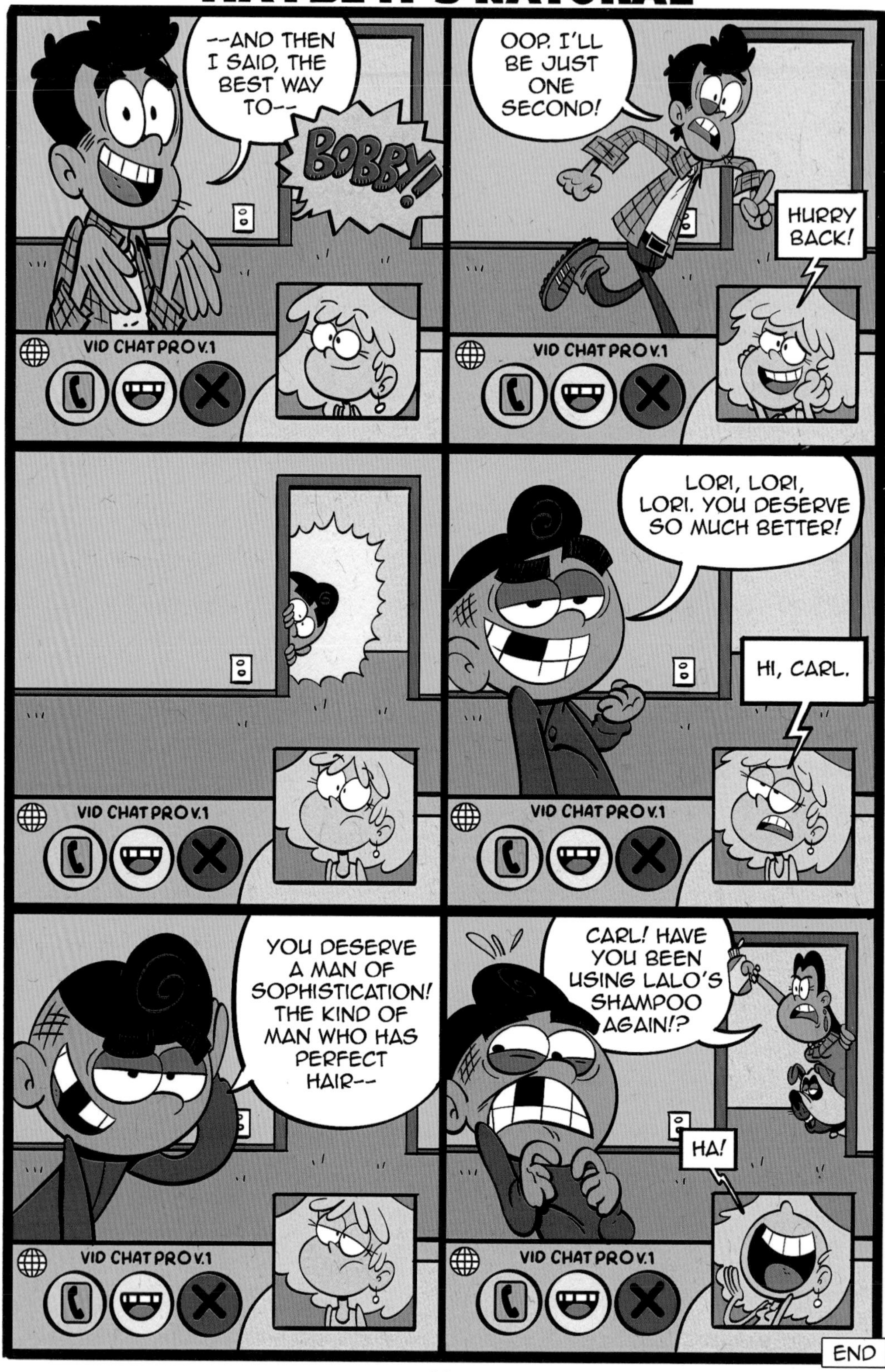

--AND THEN I SAID, THE BEST WAY TO--
BOBBY!!
VID CHAT PRO V.1
OOP. I'LL BE JUST ONE SECOND!
HURRY BACK!
VID CHAT PRO V.1
VID CHAT PRO V.1
LORI, LORI, LORI. YOU DESERVE SO MUCH BETTER!
HI, CARL.
VID CHAT PRO V.1
YOU DESERVE A MAN OF SOPHISTICATION! THE KIND OF MAN WHO HAS PERFECT HAIR--
VID CHAT PRO V.1
CARL! HAVE YOU BEEN USING LALO'S SHAMPOO AGAIN!?
HA!
VID CHAT PRO V.1
END

"SWISHFUL THINKING"

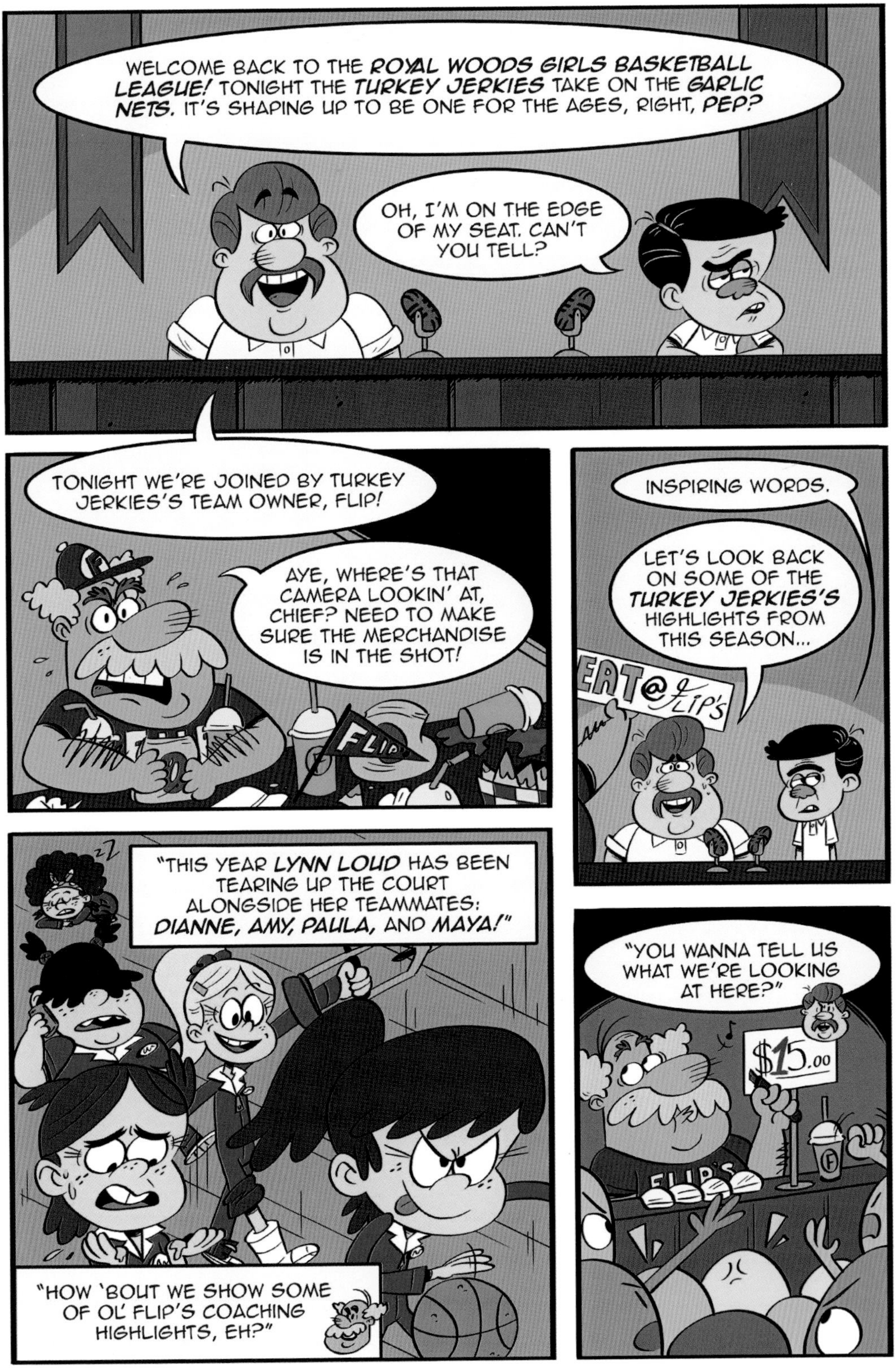

WELCOME BACK TO THE ROYAL WOODS GIRLS BASKETBALL LEAGUE! TONIGHT THE TURKEY JERKIES TAKE ON THE GARLIC NETS. IT'S SHAPING UP TO BE ONE FOR THE AGES, RIGHT, PEP?
OH, I'M ON THE EDGE OF MY SEAT. CAN'T YOU TELL?
TONIGHT WE'RE JOINED BY TURKEY JERKIES'S TEAM OWNER, FLIP!
AYE, WHERE'S THAT CAMERA LOOKIN' AT, CHIEF? NEED TO MAKE SURE THE MERCHANDISE IS IN THE SHOT!
INSPIRING WORDS.
LET'S LOOK BACK ON SOME OF THE TURKEY JERKIES'S HIGHLIGHTS FROM THIS SEASON...
EAT @ FLIP'S
"THIS YEAR LYNN LOUD HAS BEEN TEARING UP THE COURT ALONGSIDE HER TEAMMATES: DIANNE, AMY, PAULA, AND MAYA!"
"HOW 'BOUT WE SHOW SOME OF OL' FLIP'S COACHING HIGHLIGHTS, EH?"
"YOU WANNA TELL US WHAT WE'RE LOOKING AT HERE?"
$15.00

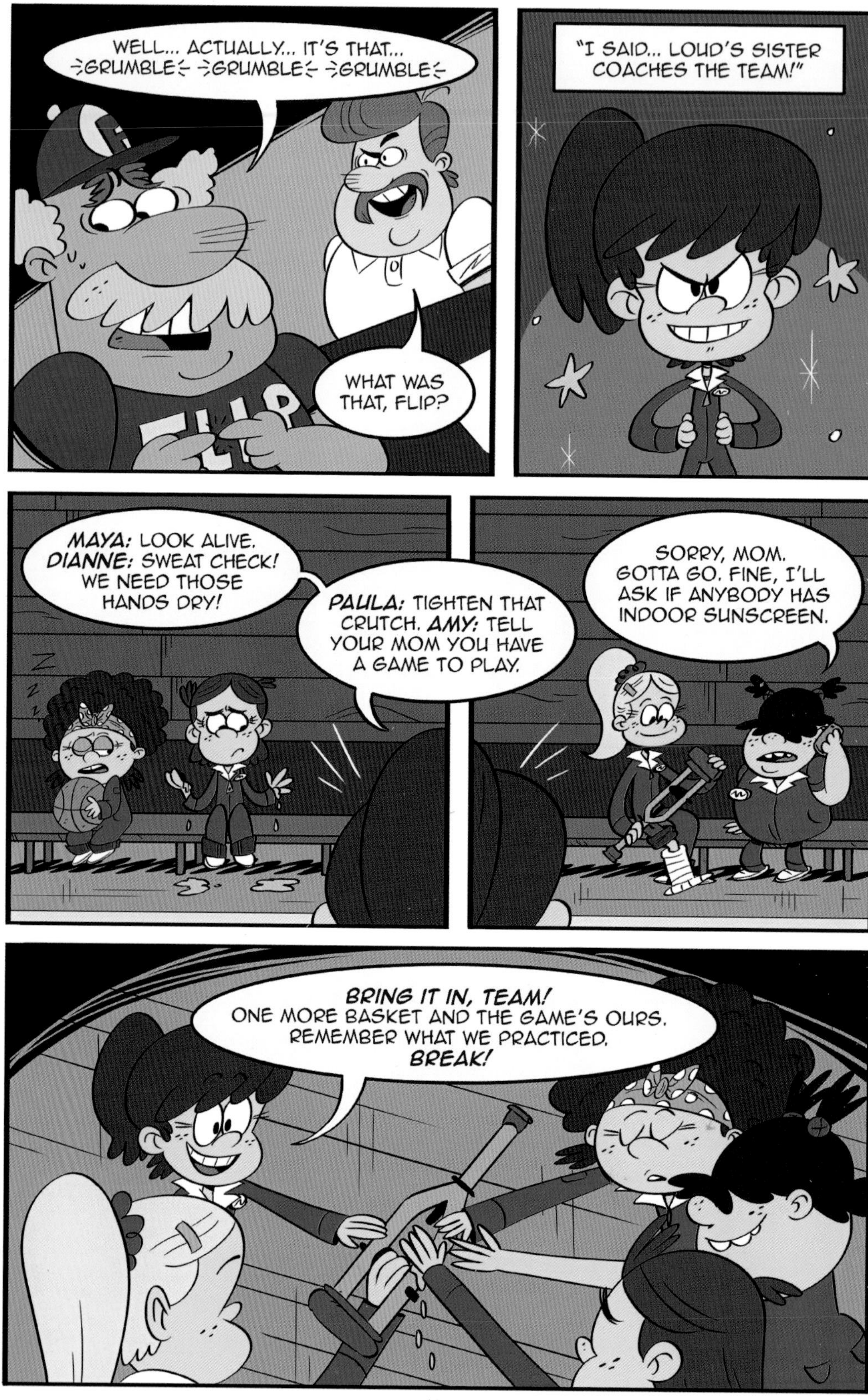
WELL... ACTUALLY... IT'S THAT... GRUMBLE GRUMBLE GRUMBLE
WHAT WAS THAT, FLIP?
"I SAID... LOUD'S SISTER COACHES THE TEAM!"
MAYA: LOOK ALIVE. DIANNE: SWEAT CHECK! WE NEED THOSE HANDS DRY!
PAULA: TIGHTEN THAT CRUTCH. AMY: TELL YOUR MOM YOU HAVE A GAME TO PLAY.
SORRY, MOM. GOTTA GO. FINE, I'LL ASK IF ANYBODY HAS INDOOR SUNSCREEN.
BRING IT IN, TEAM! ONE MORE BASKET AND THE GAME'S OURS. REMEMBER WHAT WE PRACTICED. BREAK!

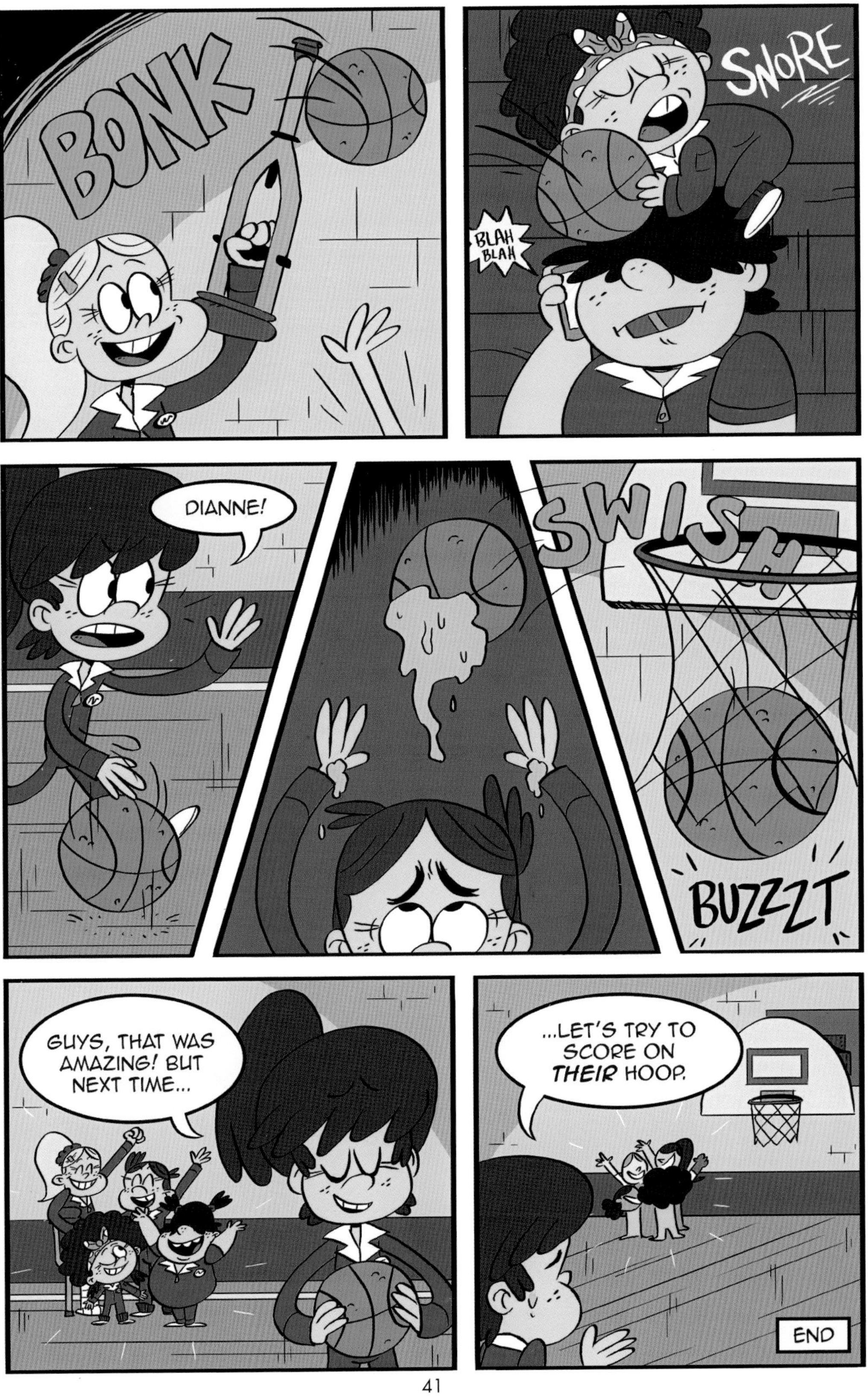

BONK
SNORE
BLAH BLAH
DIANNE!
SWISH
BUZZZT
GUYS, THAT WAS AMAZING! BUT NEXT TIME...
...LET'S TRY TO SCORE ON THEIR HOOP.
END

"SITUATION SOUFFLÉ"

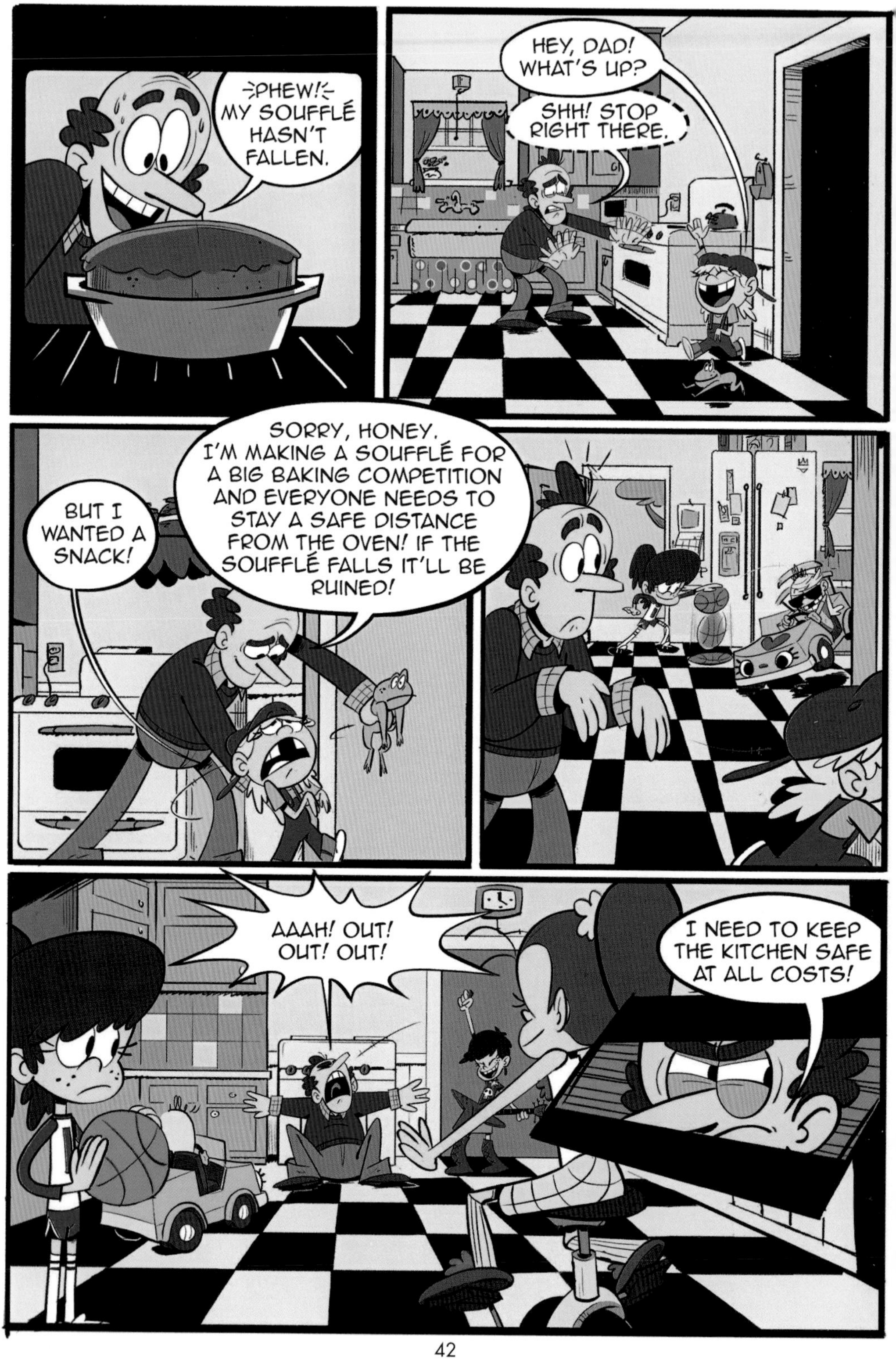
PHEW! MY SOUFFLÉ HASN'T FALLEN.
HEY, DAD! WHAT'S UP?
SHH! STOP RIGHT THERE.
BUT I WANTED A SNACK!
SORRY, HONEY. I'M MAKING A SOUFFLÉ FOR A BIG BAKING COMPETITION AND EVERYONE NEEDS TO STAY A SAFE DISTANCE FROM THE OVEN! IF THE SOUFFLÉ FALLS IT'LL BE RUINED!
AAAH! OUT! OUT! OUT!
I NEED TO KEEP THE KITCHEN SAFE AT ALL COSTS!

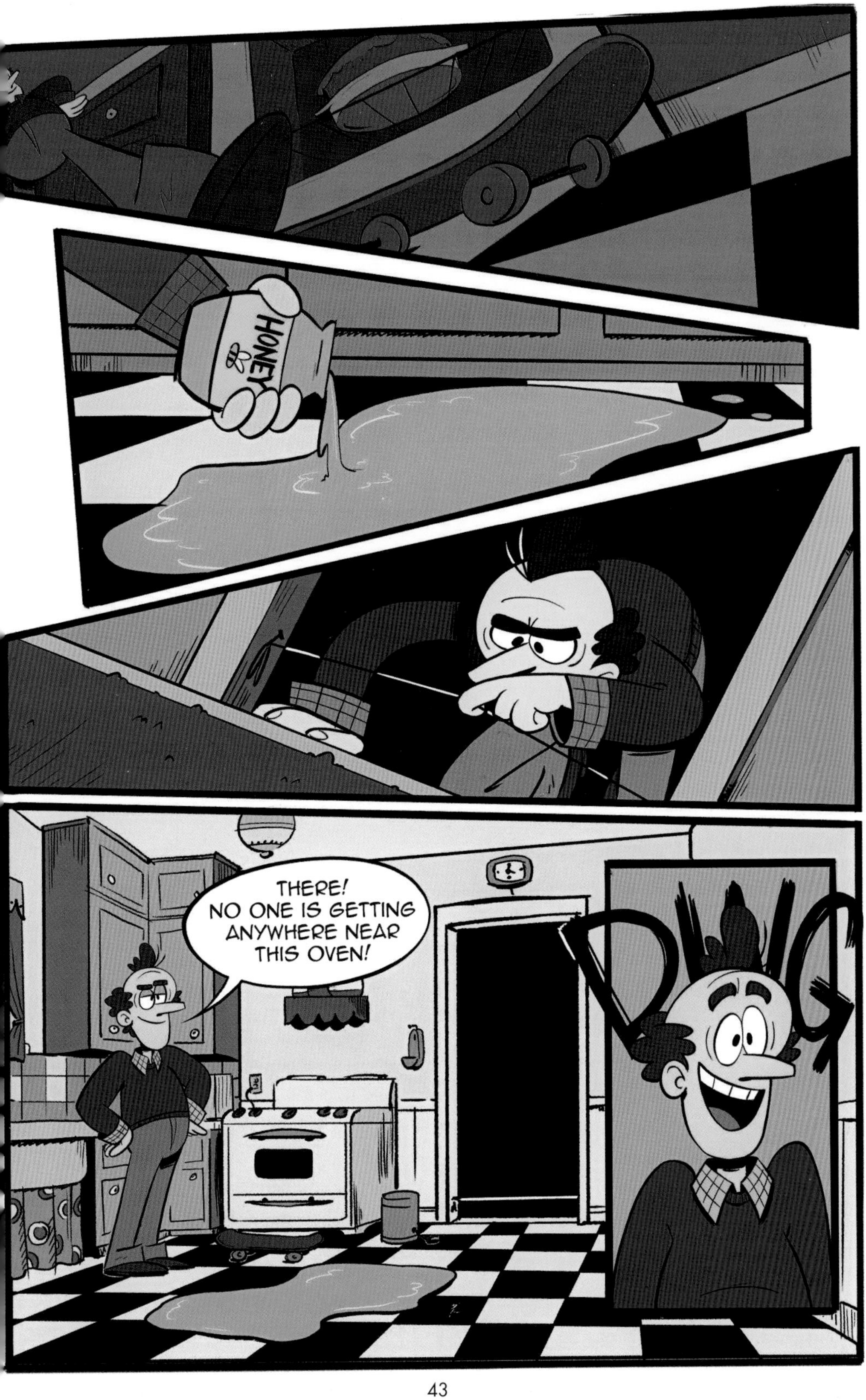
HONEY
THERE! NO ONE IS GETTING ANYWHERE NEAR THIS OVEN!
DING

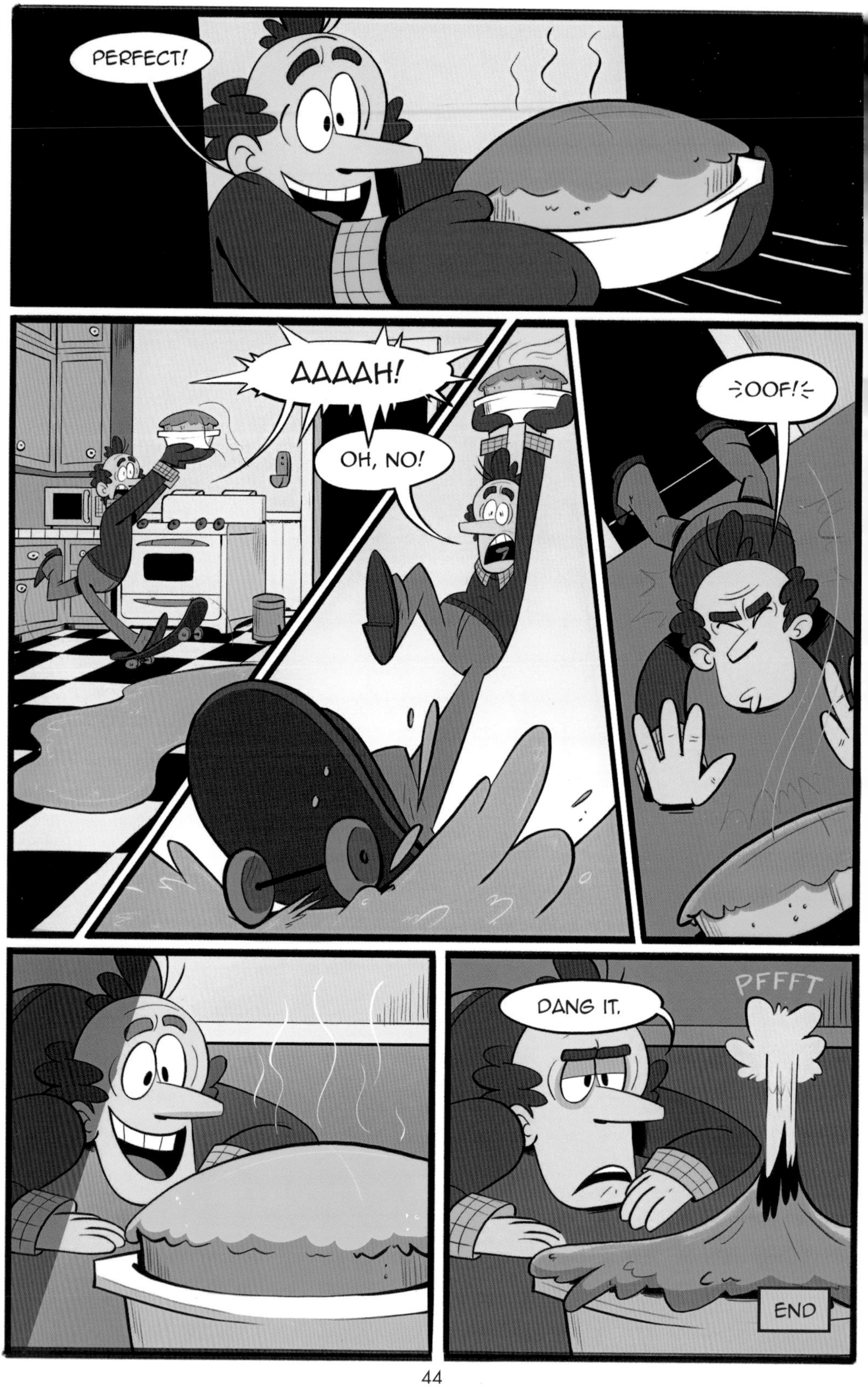
PERFECT!
AAAAH!
OH, NO!
OOF!
DANG IT.
PFFFT
END

"TOUGH HOOKY"

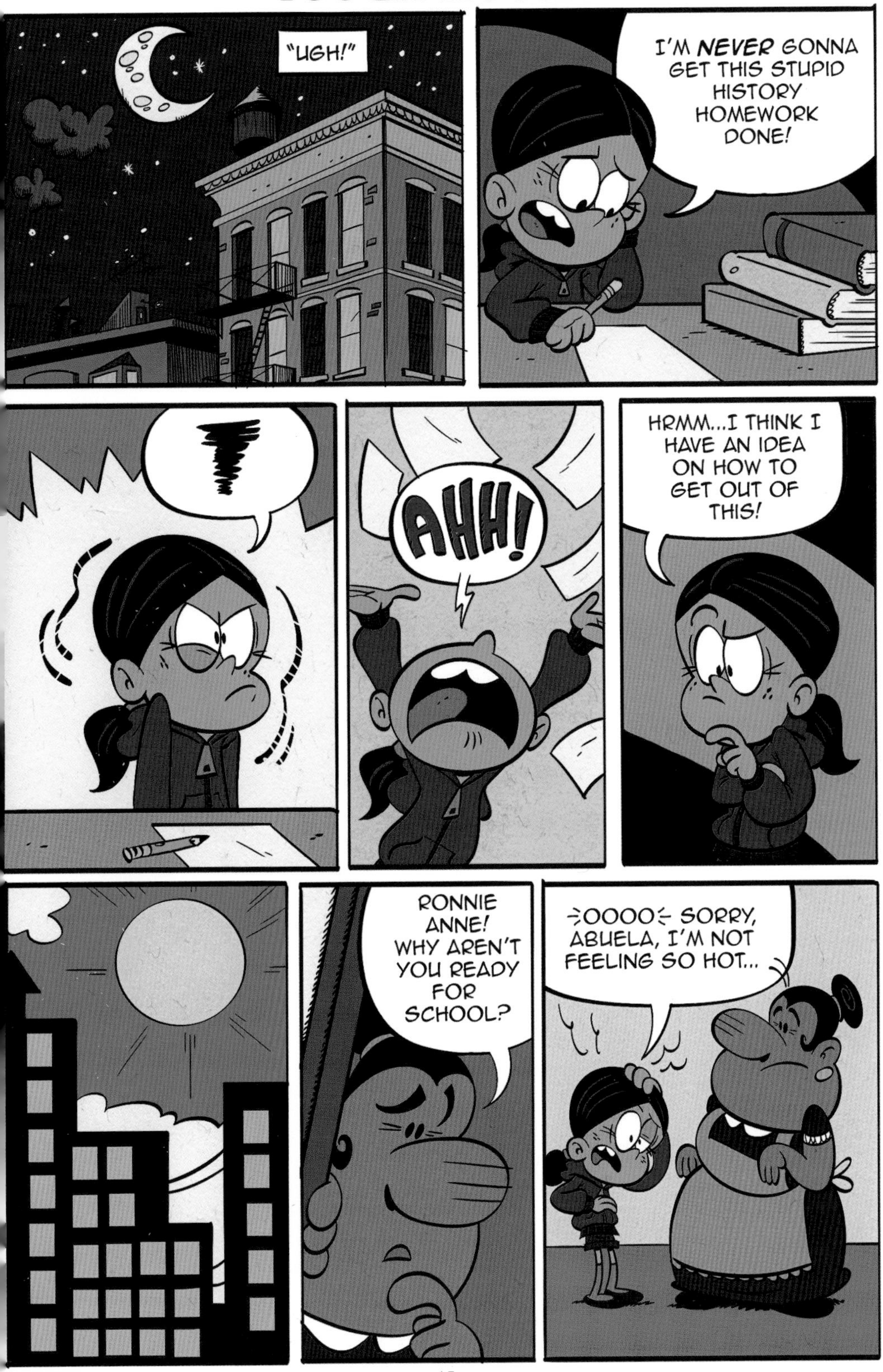

"UGH!"
I'M *NEVER* GONNA GET THIS STUPID HISTORY HOMEWORK DONE!
AHH!
HRMM...I THINK I HAVE AN IDEA ON HOW TO GET OUT OF THIS!
RONNIE ANNE! WHY AREN'T YOU READY FOR SCHOOL?
OOOO SORRY, ABUELA, I'M NOT FEELING SO HOT...

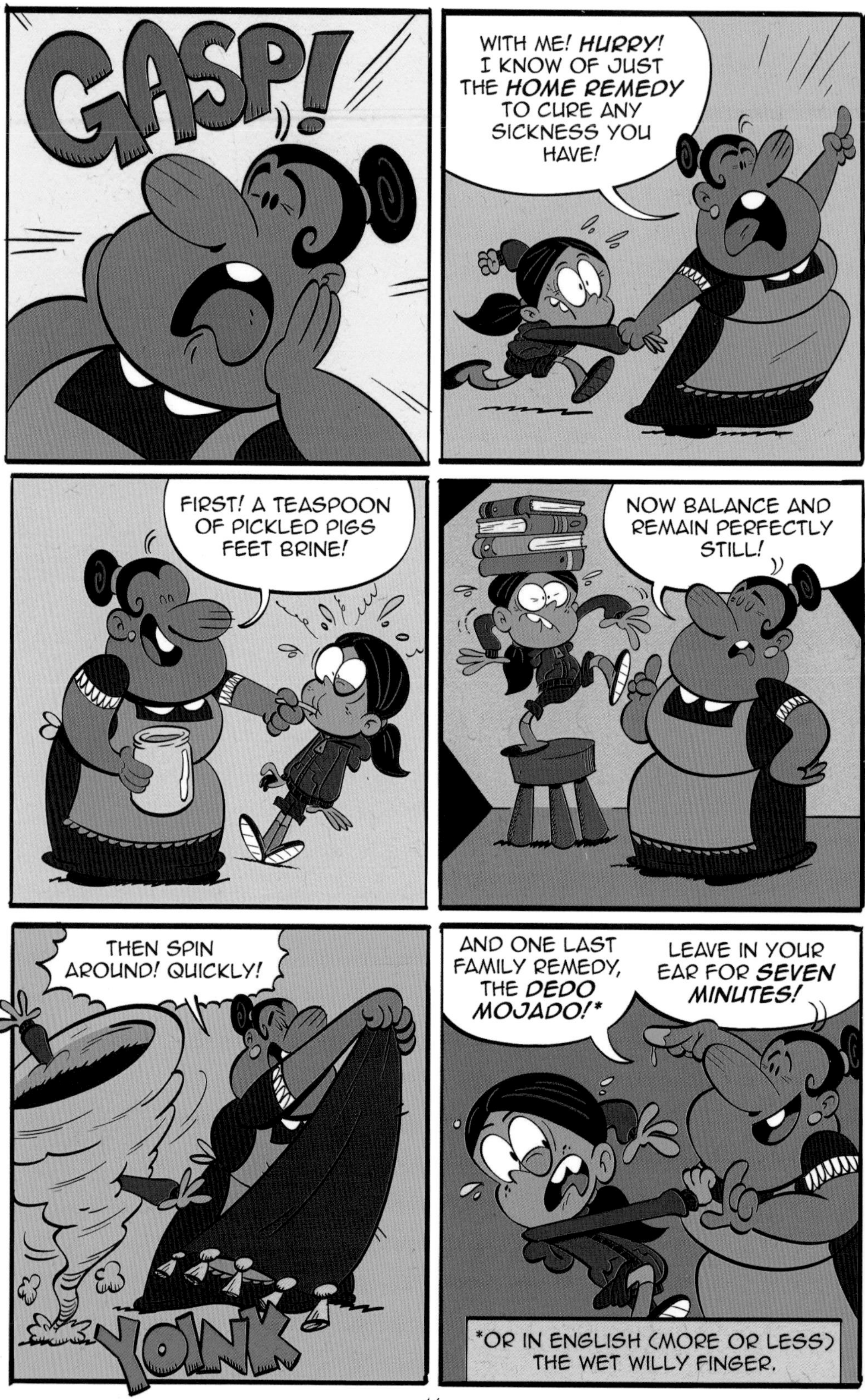
GASP!
WITH ME! HURRY! I KNOW OF JUST THE HOME REMEDY TO CURE ANY SICKNESS YOU HAVE!
FIRST! A TEASPOON OF PICKLED PIGS FEET BRINE!
NOW BALANCE AND REMAIN PERFECTLY STILL!
THEN SPIN AROUND! QUICKLY!
YOINK
AND ONE LAST FAMILY REMEDY, THE DEDO MOJADO!*
LEAVE IN YOUR EAR FOR SEVEN MINUTES!
*OR IN ENGLISH (MORE OR LESS) THE WET WILLY FINGER.

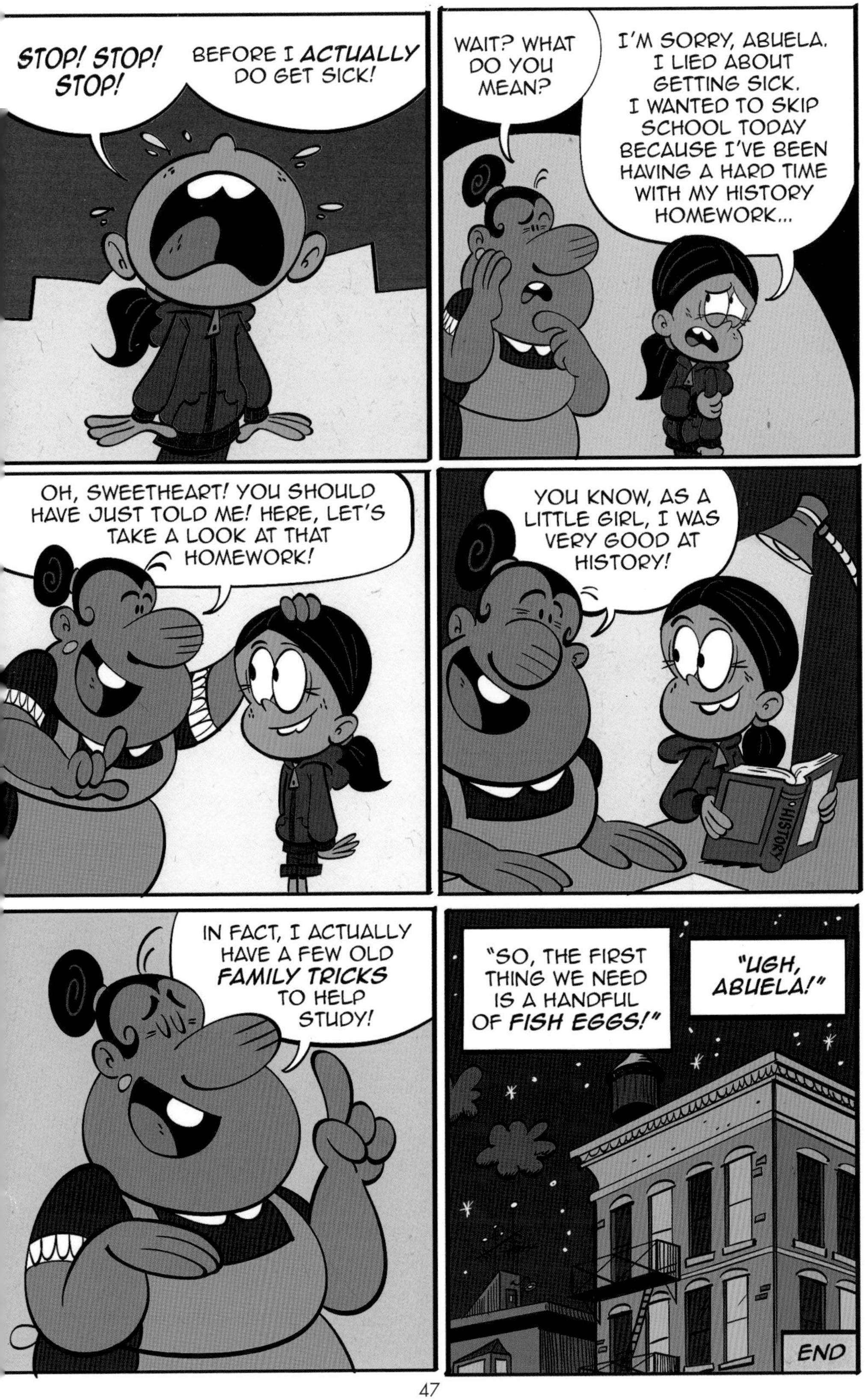
STOP! STOP! STOP!
BEFORE I ACTUALLY DO GET SICK!
WAIT? WHAT DO YOU MEAN?
I'M SORRY, ABUELA. I LIED ABOUT GETTING SICK. I WANTED TO SKIP SCHOOL TODAY BECAUSE I'VE BEEN HAVING A HARD TIME WITH MY HISTORY HOMEWORK...
OH, SWEETHEART! YOU SHOULD HAVE JUST TOLD ME! HERE, LET'S TAKE A LOOK AT THAT HOMEWORK!
YOU KNOW, AS A LITTLE GIRL, I WAS VERY GOOD AT HISTORY!
HISTORY
IN FACT, I ACTUALLY HAVE A FEW OLD FAMILY TRICKS TO HELP STUDY!
"SO, THE FIRST THING WE NEED IS A HANDFUL OF FISH EGGS!"
"UGH, ABUELA!"
END

"SORE PLAYERS"

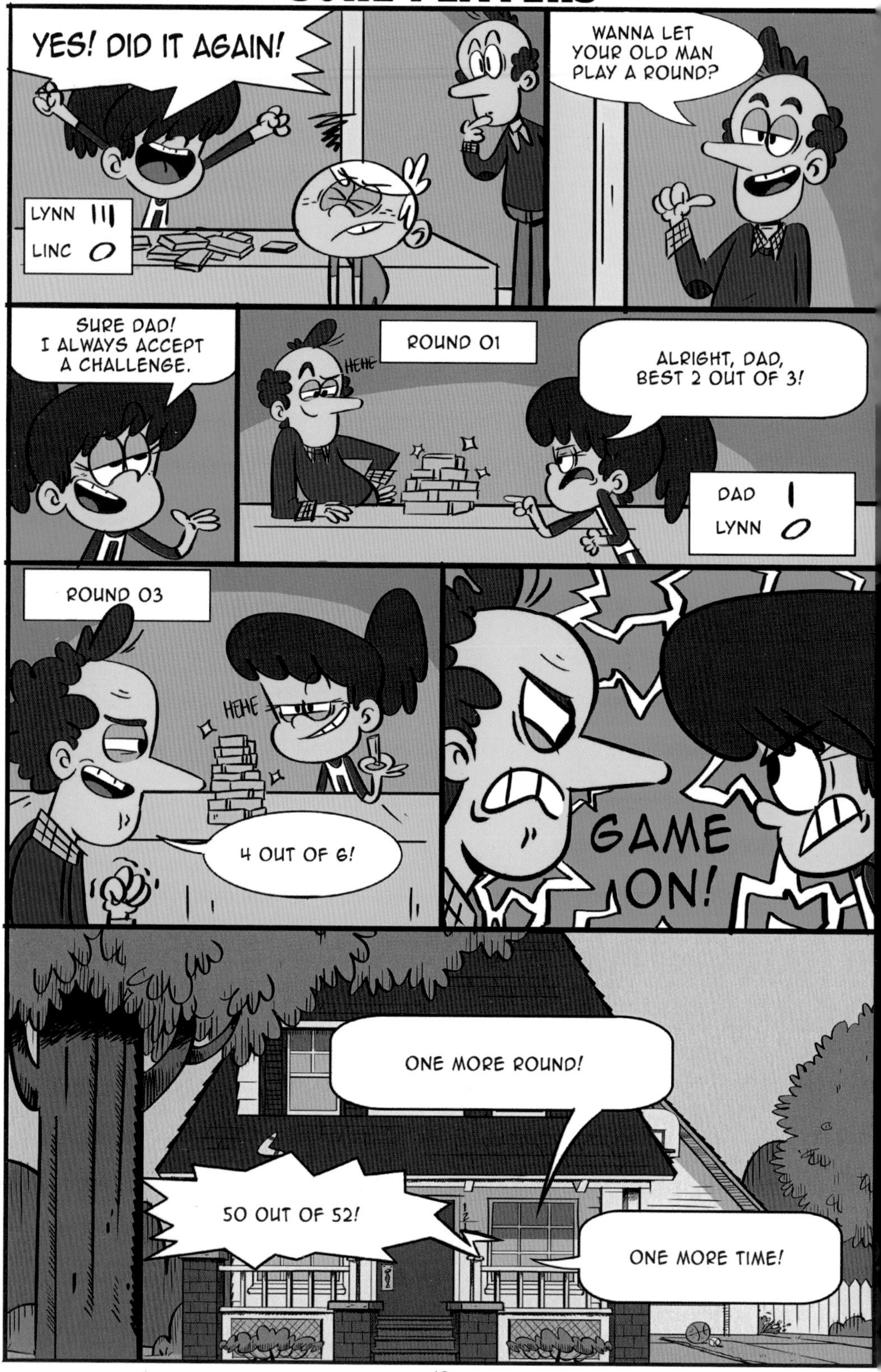

YES! DID IT AGAIN!
LYNN III
LINC 0
WANNA LET YOUR OLD MAN PLAY A ROUND?
SURE DAD! I ALWAYS ACCEPT A CHALLENGE.
ROUND 01
HEHE
ALRIGHT, DAD, BEST 2 OUT OF 3!
DAD 1
LYNN 0
ROUND 03
HEHE
4 OUT OF 6!
GAME ON!
ONE MORE ROUND!
50 OUT OF 52!
ONE MORE TIME!

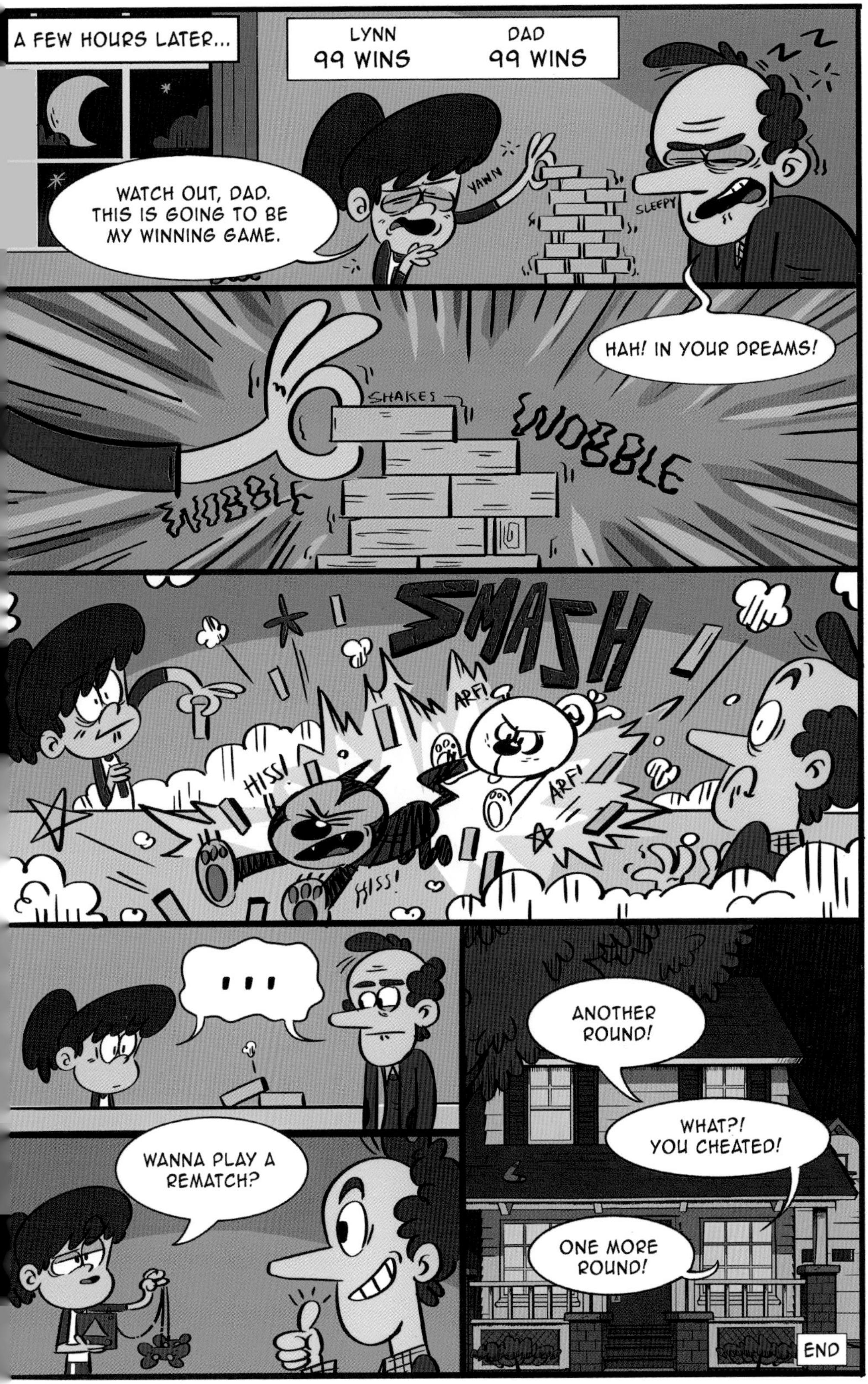
A FEW HOURS LATER...
LYNN 99 WINS
DAD 99 WINS
WATCH OUT, DAD. THIS IS GOING TO BE MY WINNING GAME.
YAWN
SLEEPY
HAH! IN YOUR DREAMS!
SHAKES
WOBBLE
WOBBLE
SMASH!
ARF!
HISS!
ARF!
HISS!
...
ANOTHER ROUND!
WANNA PLAY A REMATCH?
WHAT?! YOU CHEATED!
ONE MORE ROUND!
END

"CITIZEN LOUD"

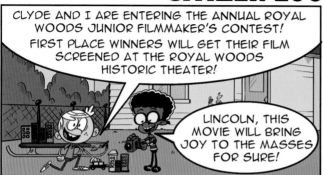

CLYDE AND I ARE ENTERING THE ANNUAL ROYAL WOODS JUNIOR FILMMAKER'S CONTEST! FIRST PLACE WINNERS WILL GET THEIR FILM SCREENED AT THE ROYAL WOODS HISTORIC THEATER!

LINCOLN, THIS MOVIE WILL BRING JOY TO THE MASSES FOR SURE!

CLINCOLN McCLOUD: THE MOVIE!

LET'S DO IT!

ACTION!

LYNN LOUD SHOOTS AND SHE SCORES!

BONK

DANG IT, LYNN! YOU RUINED OUR TAKE!

STINKIN', YOU MADE ME FOUL!

LET'S TRY THIS AGAIN.

ACTION!

SNARL!

AAUUUGGGHHHH!

AWWW, THERE YOU ARE, *BITEY!* IT'S TIME FOR YOUR MUD BATH!

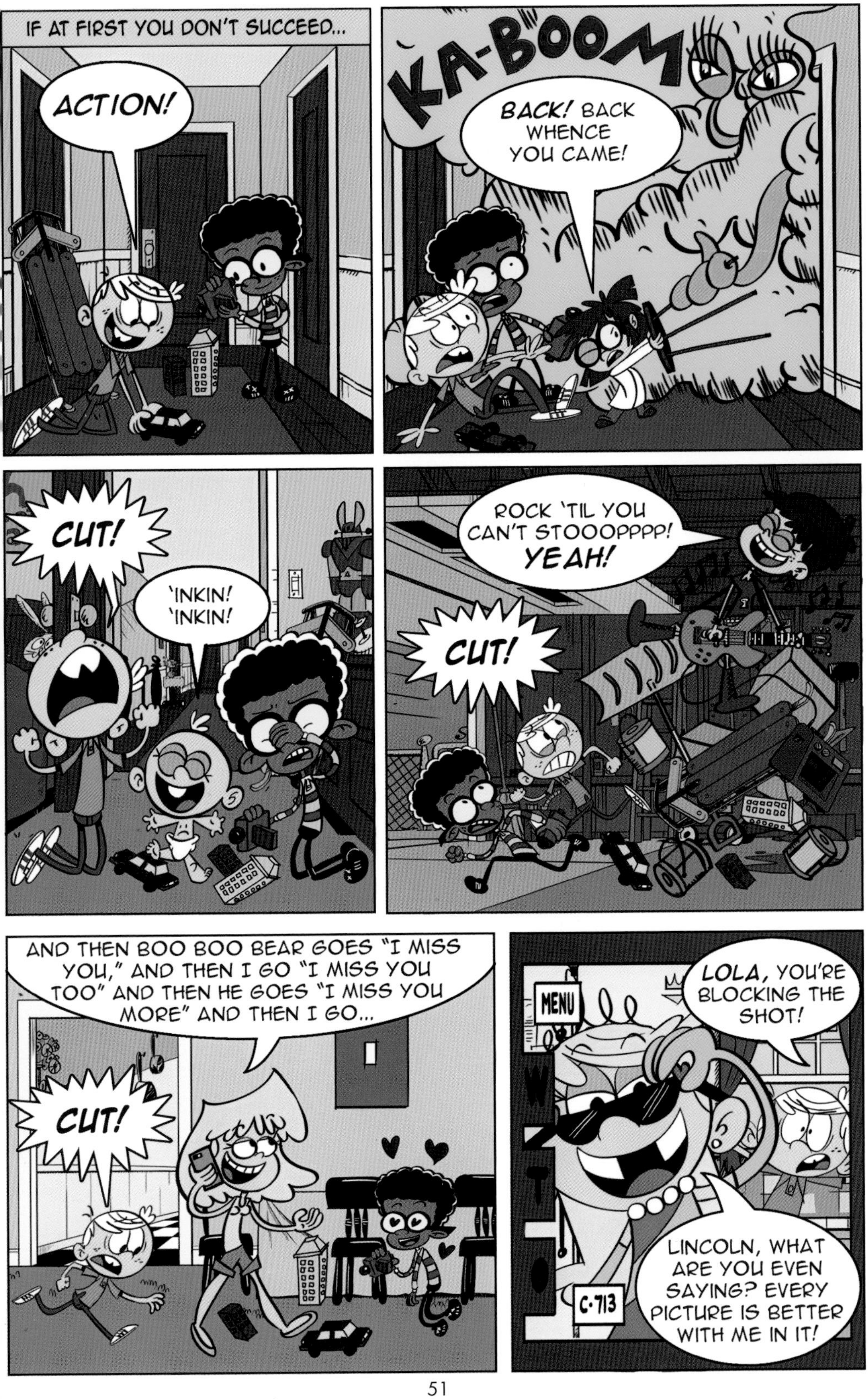
IF AT FIRST YOU DON'T SUCCEED...
ACTION!
KA-BOOM
BACK! BACK WHENCE YOU CAME!
CUT!
'INKIN! 'INKIN!
ROCK 'TIL YOU CAN'T STOOOPPPP! YEAH!
CUT!
AND THEN BOO BOO BEAR GOES "I MISS YOU," AND THEN I GO "I MISS YOU TOO" AND THEN HE GOES "I MISS YOU MORE" AND THEN I GO...
CUT!
MENU
LOLA, YOU'RE BLOCKING THE SHOT!
C-713
LINCOLN, WHAT ARE YOU EVEN SAYING? EVERY PICTURE IS BETTER WITH ME IN IT!

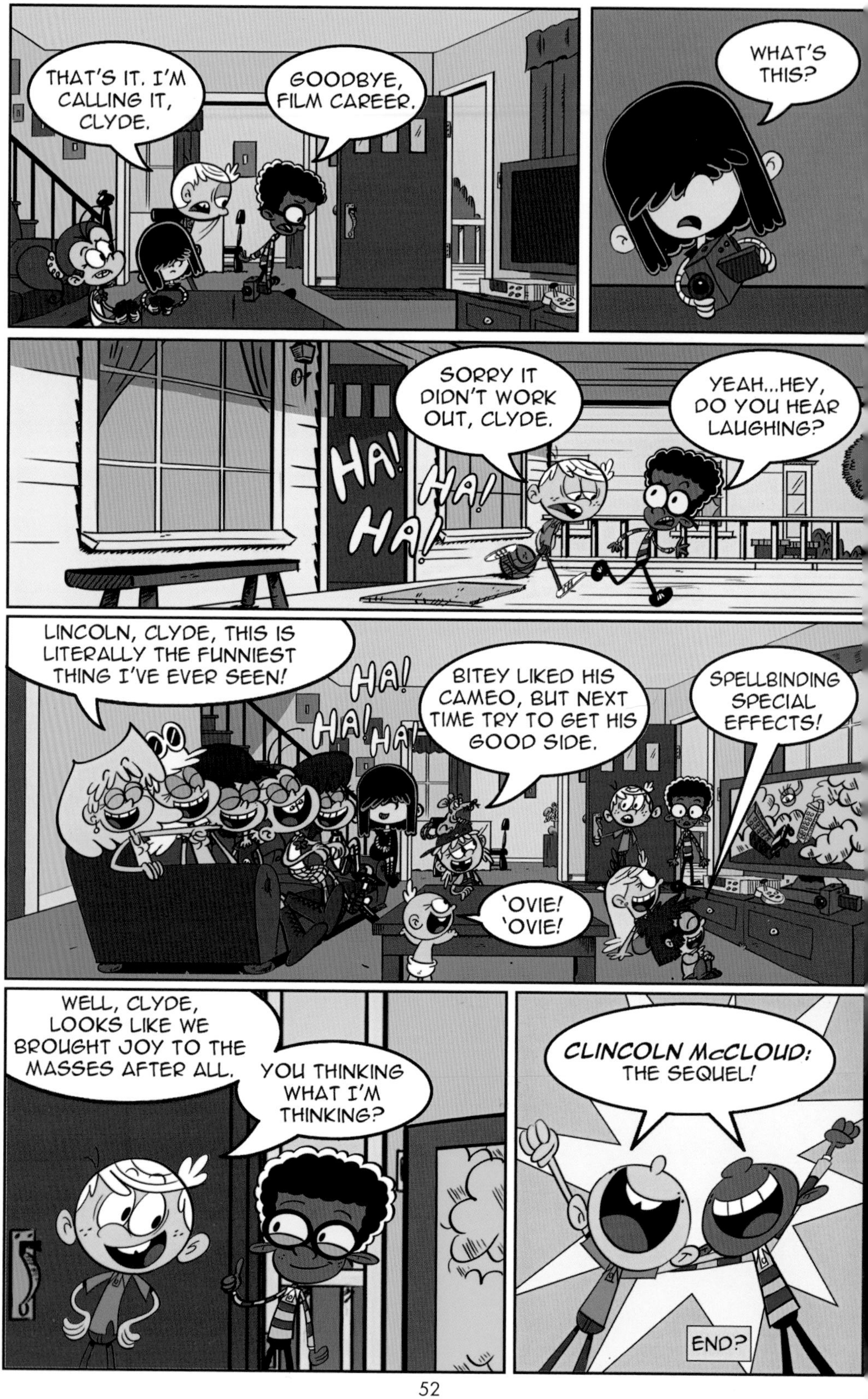
THAT'S IT. I'M CALLING IT, CLYDE.
GOODBYE, FILM CAREER.
WHAT'S THIS?
SORRY IT DIDN'T WORK OUT, CLYDE.
HA! HA! HA!
YEAH...HEY, DO YOU HEAR LAUGHING?
LINCOLN, CLYDE, THIS IS LITERALLY THE FUNNIEST THING I'VE EVER SEEN!
HA! HA! HA!
BITEY LIKED HIS CAMEO, BUT NEXT TIME TRY TO GET HIS GOOD SIDE.
SPELLBINDING SPECIAL EFFECTS!
'OVIE! 'OVIE!
WELL, CLYDE, LOOKS LIKE WE BROUGHT JOY TO THE MASSES AFTER ALL.
YOU THINKING WHAT I'M THINKING?
CLINCOLN McCLOUD: THE SEQUEL!
END?

"BABY BREAK"

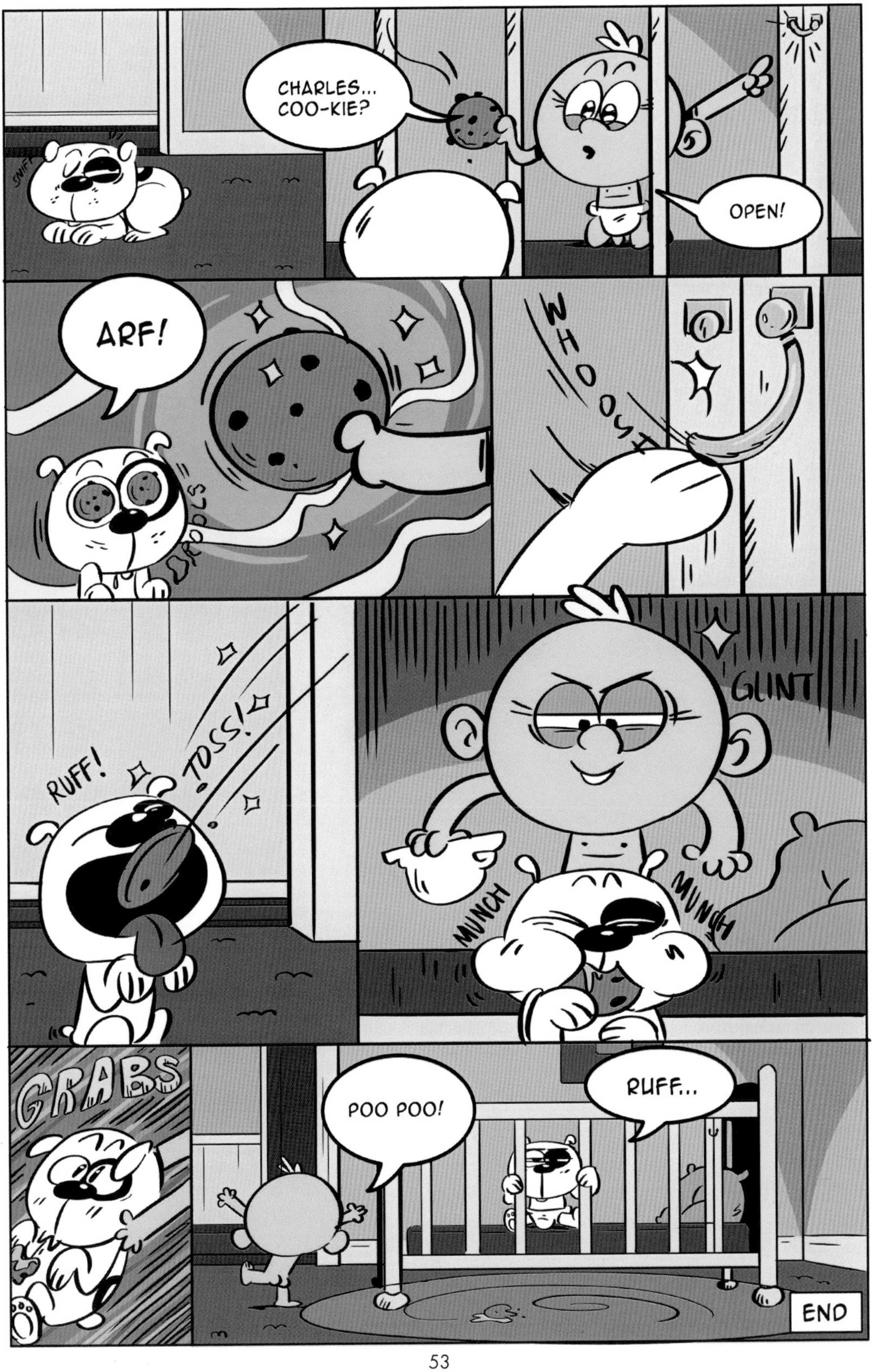
SNIFF
CHARLES... COO-KIE?
OPEN!
ARF!
DROOLS
WHOOOSH
RUFF!
TOSS!
GLINT
MUNCH
MUNCH
GRABS
POO POO!
RUFF...
END

"LEAVE A PENNY, TAKE A PENNY"

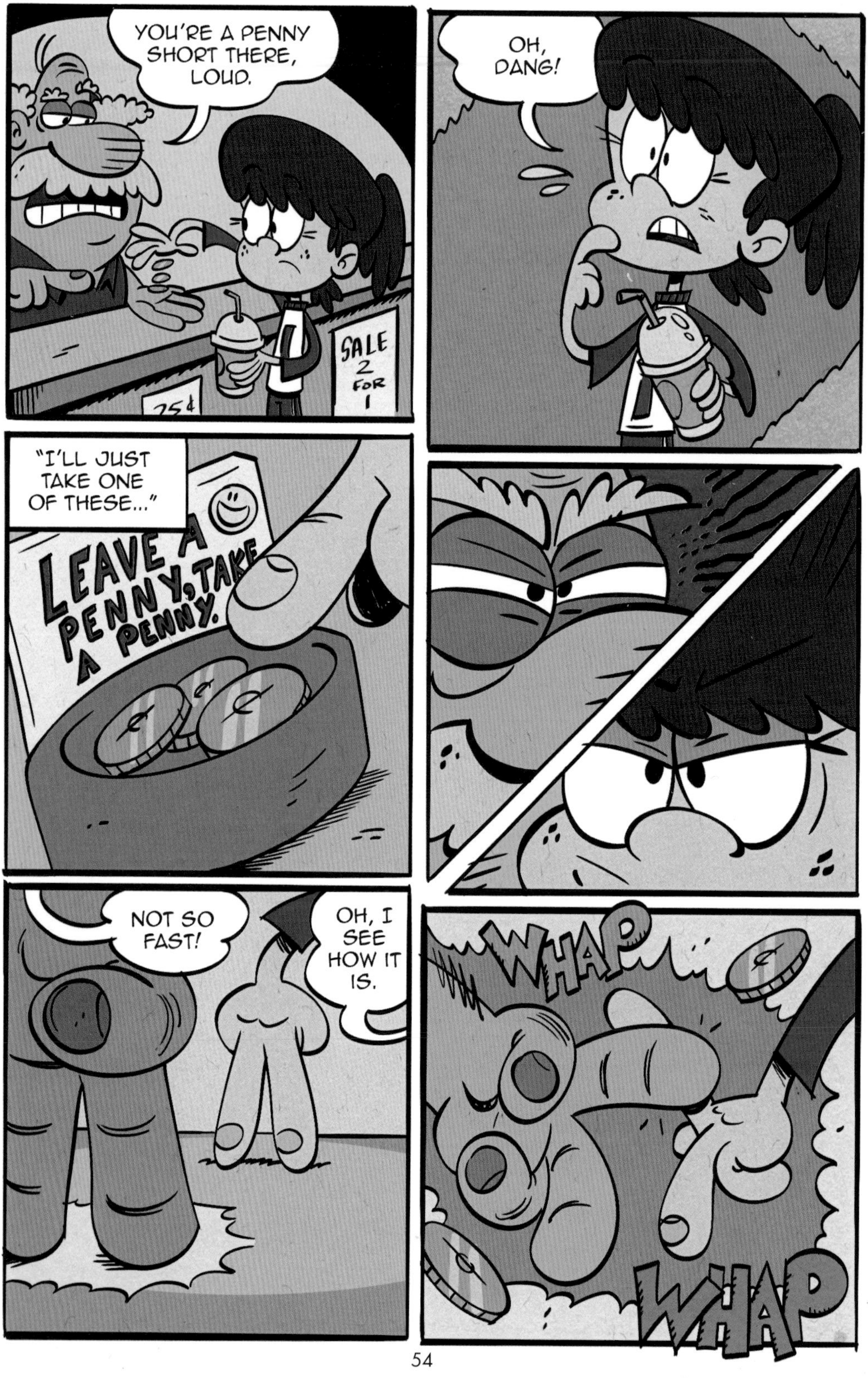
YOU'RE A PENNY SHORT THERE, LOUD.
SALE 2 FOR 1
25¢
OH, DANG!
"I'LL JUST TAKE ONE OF THESE..."
LEAVE A PENNY, TAKE A PENNY.
NOT SO FAST!
OH, I SEE HOW IT IS.
WHAP
WHAP

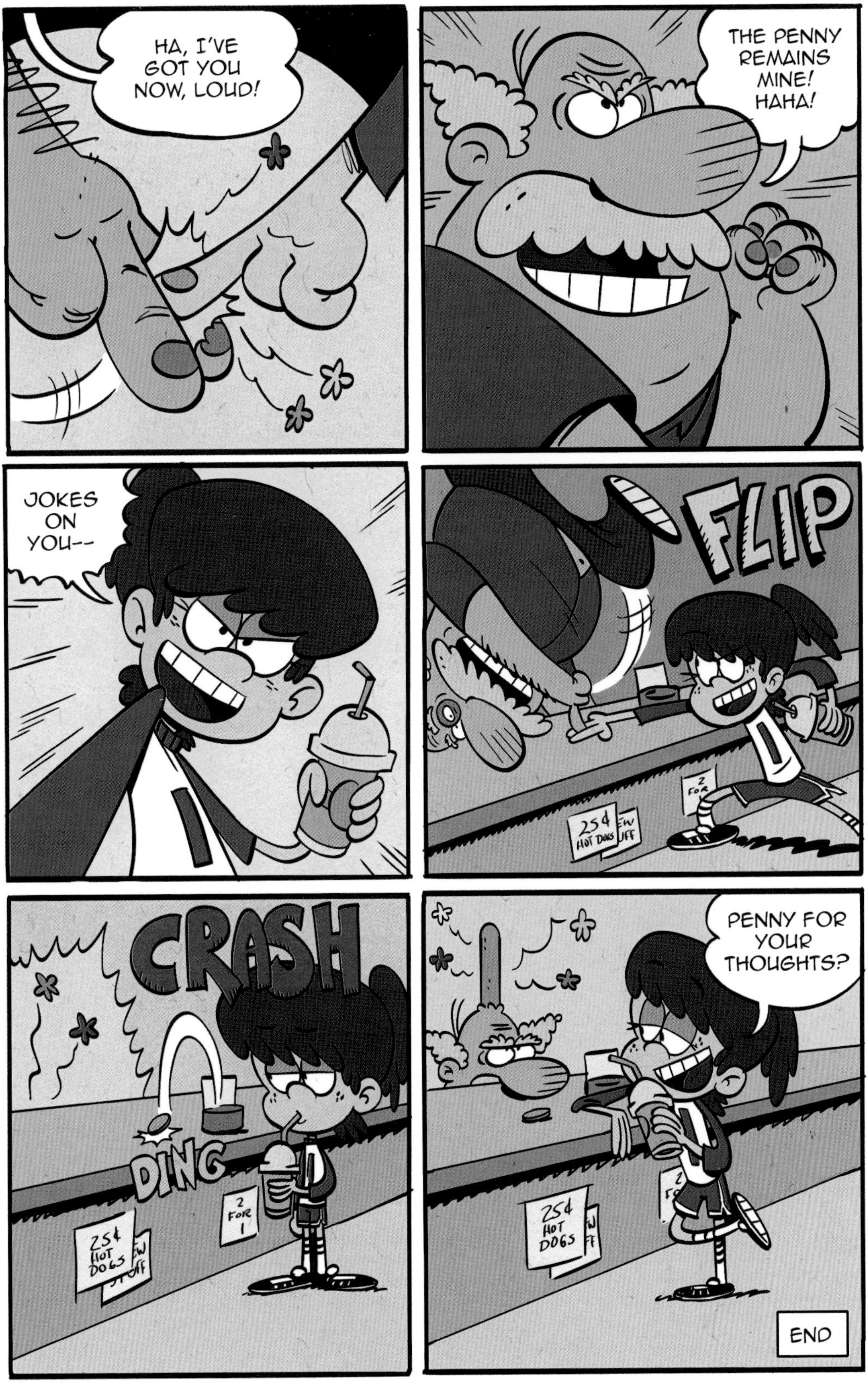
HA, I'VE GOT YOU NOW, LOUD!
THE PENNY REMAINS MINE! HAHA!
JOKES ON YOU--
FLIP
25¢ HOT DOGS
CRASH
DING
2 FOR 1
25¢ HOT DOGS
PENNY FOR YOUR THOUGHTS?
25¢ HOT DOGS
END

"DRESSED OUT"

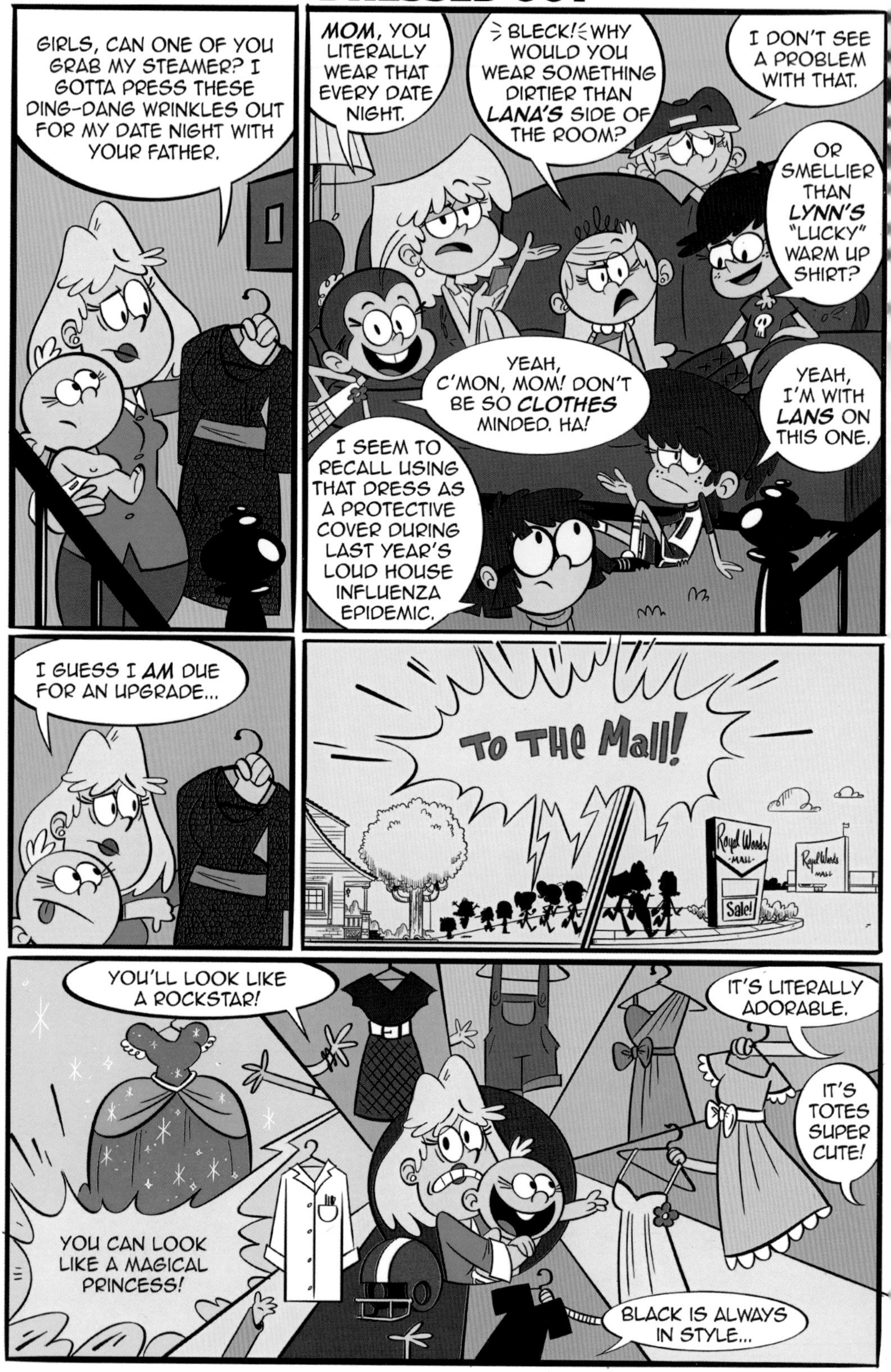
GIRLS, CAN ONE OF YOU GRAB MY STEAMER? I GOTTA PRESS THESE DING-DANG WRINKLES OUT FOR MY DATE NIGHT WITH YOUR FATHER.
MOM, YOU LITERALLY WEAR THAT EVERY DATE NIGHT.
BLECK! WHY WOULD YOU WEAR SOMETHING DIRTIER THAN LANA'S SIDE OF THE ROOM?
I DON'T SEE A PROBLEM WITH THAT.
OR SMELLIER THAN LYNN'S "LUCKY" WARM UP SHIRT?
YEAH, C'MON, MOM! DON'T BE SO CLOTHES MINDED. HA!
YEAH, I'M WITH LANS ON THIS ONE.
I SEEM TO RECALL USING THAT DRESS AS A PROTECTIVE COVER DURING LAST YEAR'S LOUD HOUSE INFLUENZA EPIDEMIC.
I GUESS I AM DUE FOR AN UPGRADE...
To THE Mall!
Royal Woods MALL
Sale!
Royal Woods MALL
YOU'LL LOOK LIKE A ROCKSTAR!
IT'S LITERALLY ADORABLE.
IT'S TOTES SUPER CUTE!
YOU CAN LOOK LIKE A MAGICAL PRINCESS!
BLACK IS ALWAYS IN STYLE...

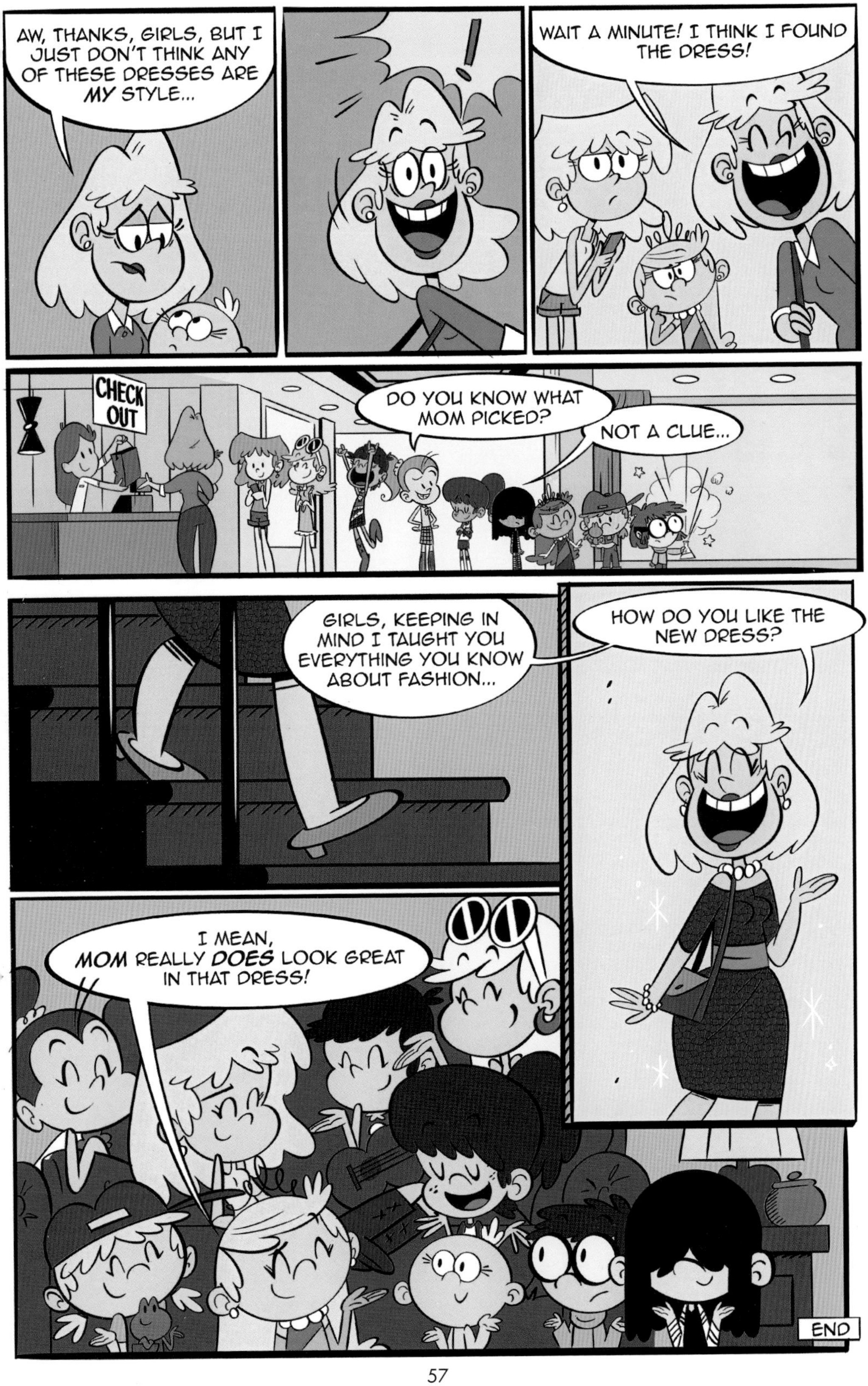
AW, THANKS, GIRLS, BUT I JUST DON'T THINK ANY OF THESE DRESSES ARE *MY* STYLE...
!
WAIT A MINUTE! I THINK I FOUND THE DRESS!
CHECK OUT
DO YOU KNOW WHAT MOM PICKED?
NOT A CLUE...
GIRLS, KEEPING IN MIND I TAUGHT YOU EVERYTHING YOU KNOW ABOUT FASHION...
HOW DO YOU LIKE THE NEW DRESS?
I MEAN, ***MOM*** REALLY ***DOES*** LOOK GREAT IN THAT DRESS!
END

"LUCY'S ABCs OF THE LOUD HOUSE"

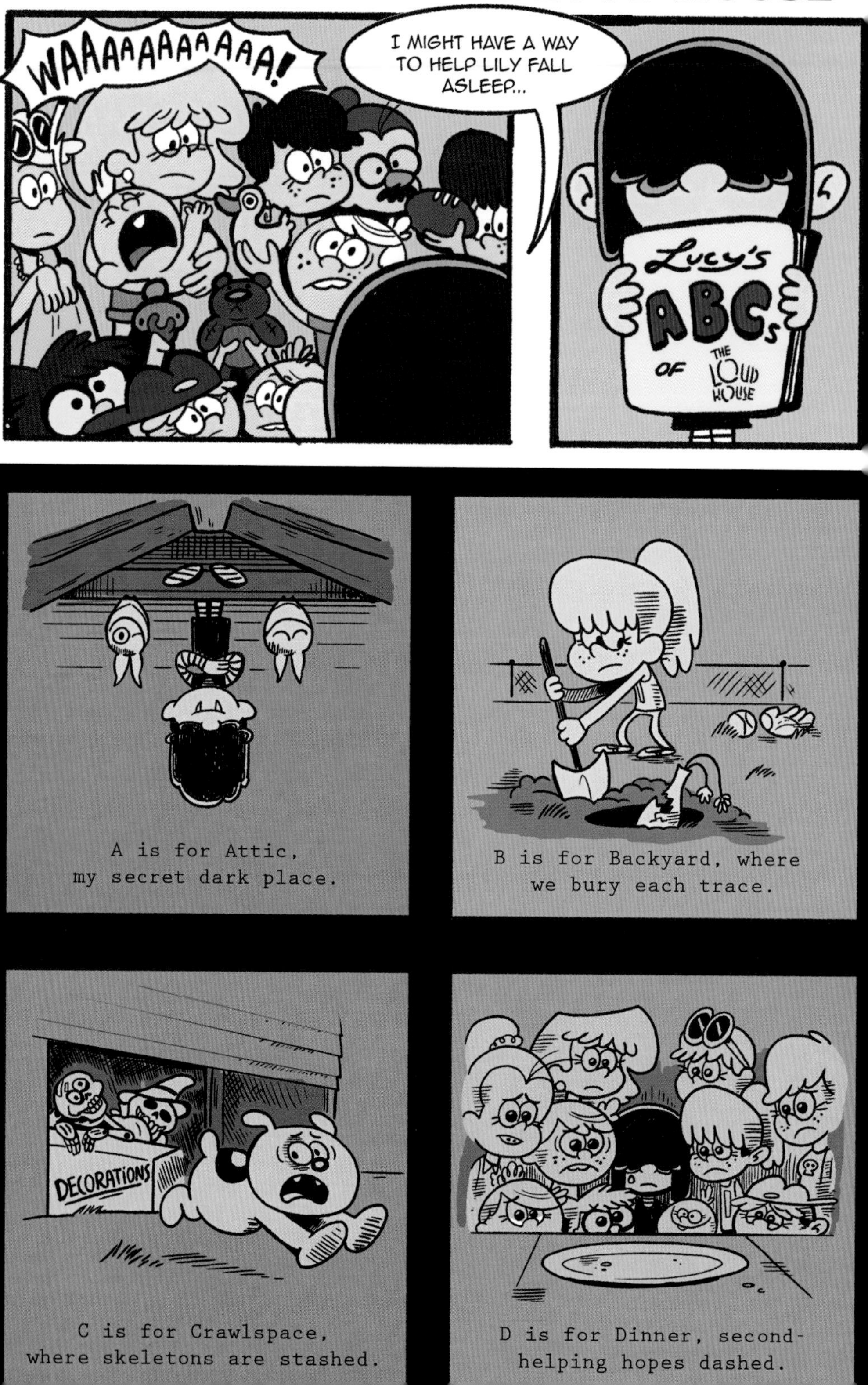
WAAAAAAAAAAA!
I MIGHT HAVE A WAY TO HELP LILY FALL ASLEEP...
Lucy's ABCs OF THE LOUD HOUSE
A is for Attic, my secret dark place.
B is for Backyard, where we bury each trace.
DECORATIONS
C is for Crawlspace, where skeletons are stashed.
D is for Dinner, second-helping hopes dashed.

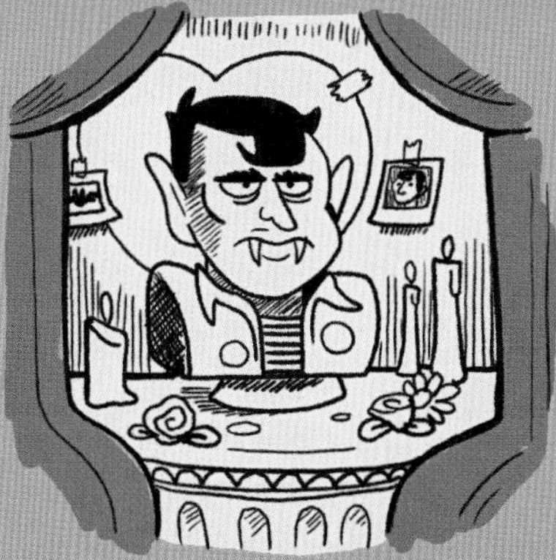

E is for Edwin shrine,
safe in my room.

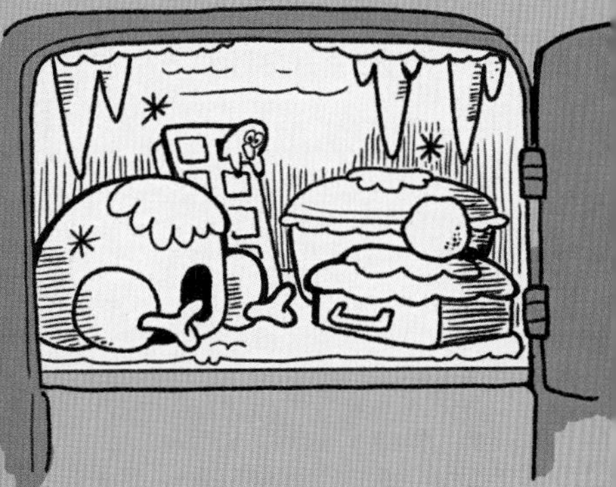

F is for Freezer, where
leftovers meet their doom.

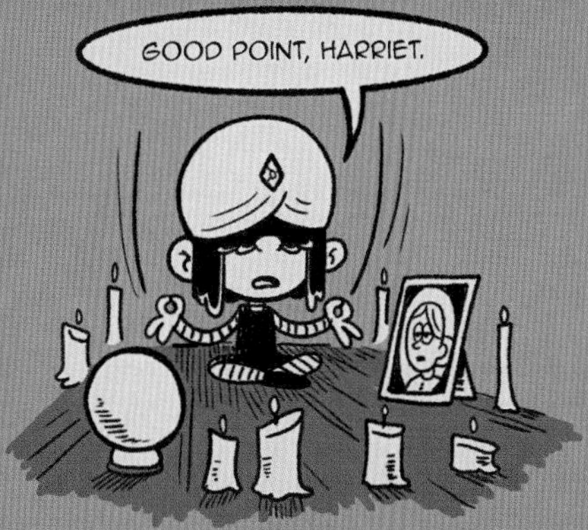
GOOD POINT, HARRIET.

G is for Great Grandma,
of whom I'm so fond.

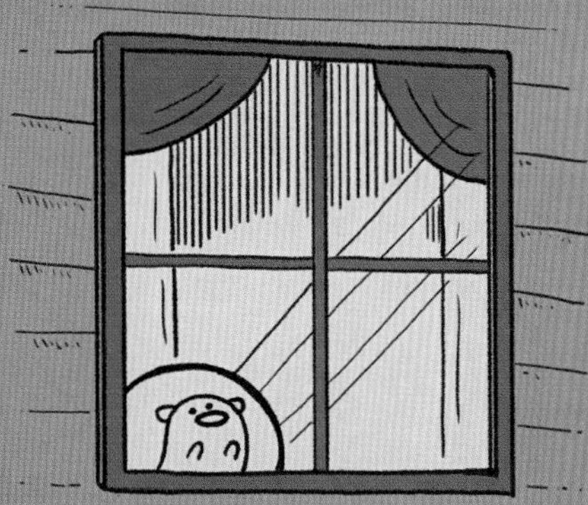

H is for Hamster ball,
Geo can't get beyond.

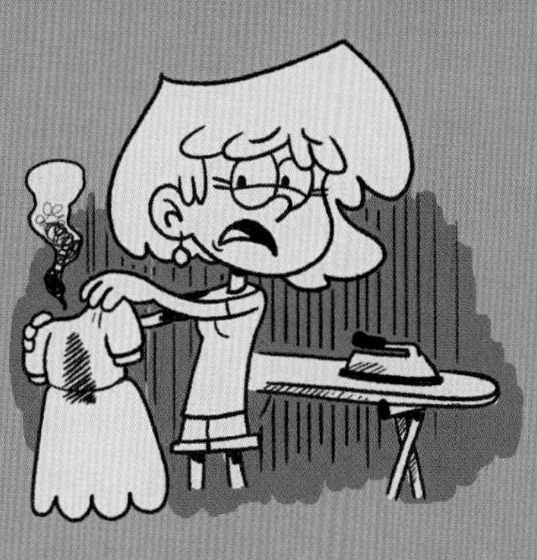

I is for Iron,
feared by our clothes.

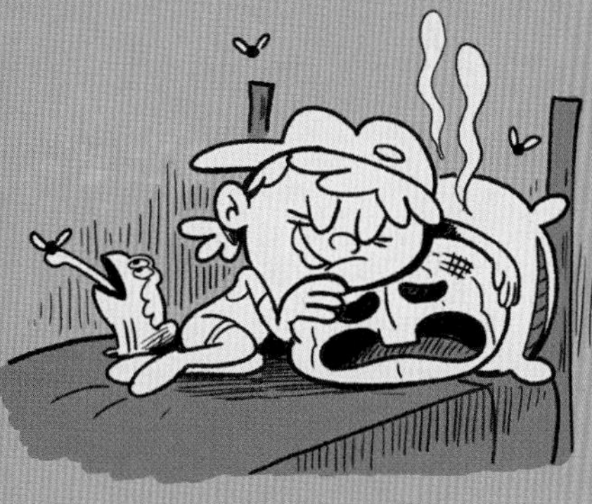

J is for Jack-O-Lantern
that got really gross.

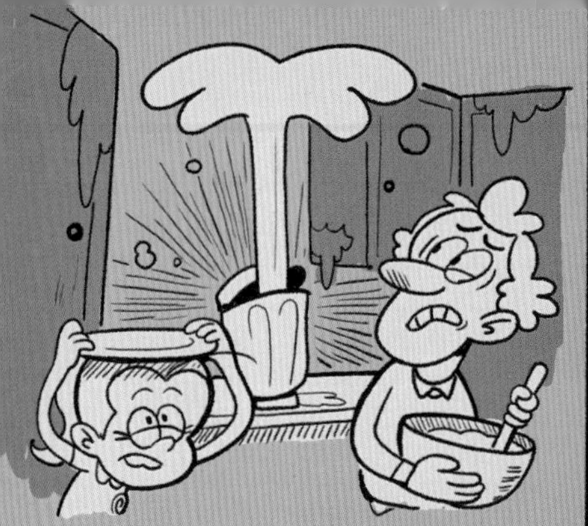

K is for Kitchen,
whose hazards are various.

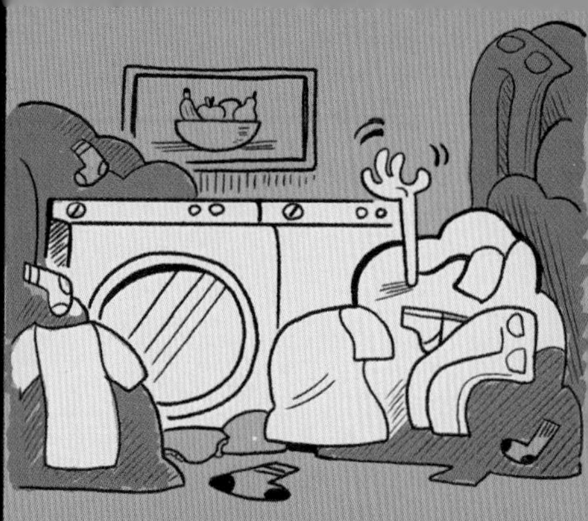

L is for Laundry that
threatens to bury us.

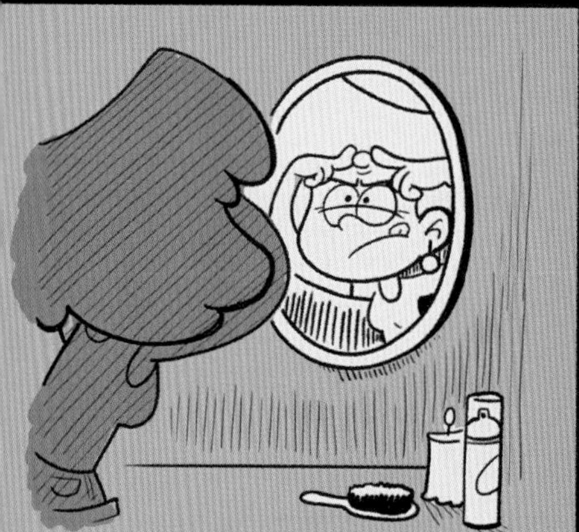

M is for Mirror and
the horrors it's seen.

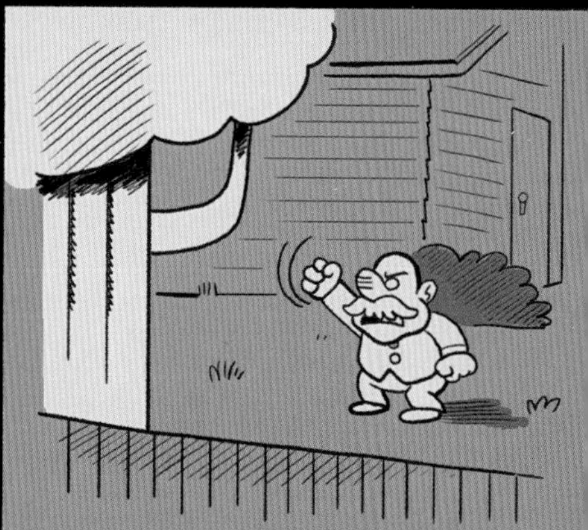

N is for Next-door neighbors
who're totally mean.

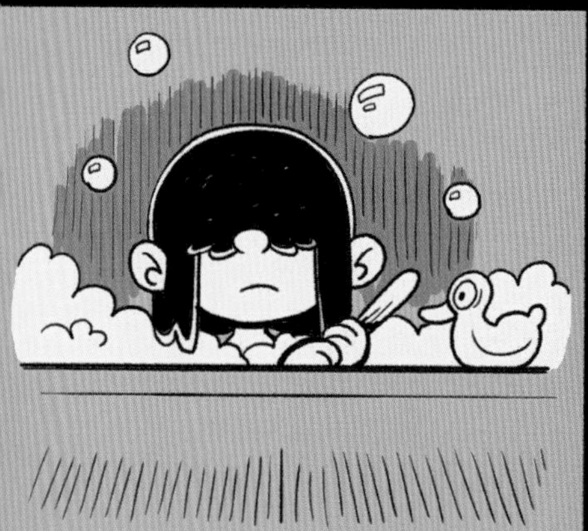

O is for Omens, which I
see in my bubble brew.

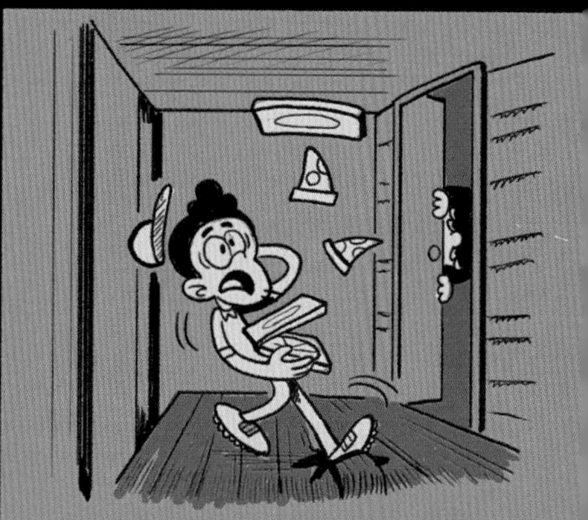

P is for Porch boards,
rotted right through.

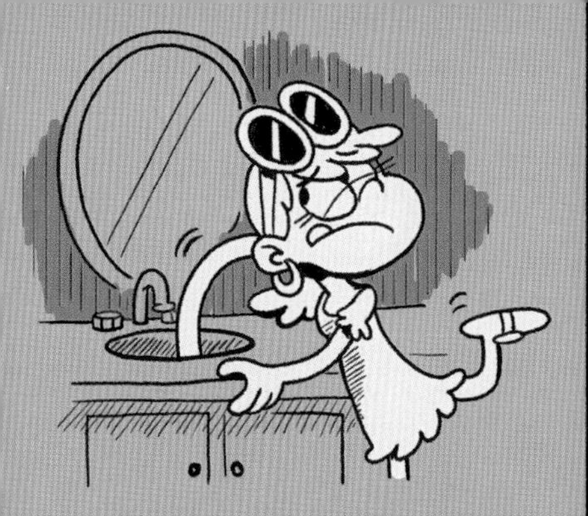

Q is for Quarters
lost down the drain.

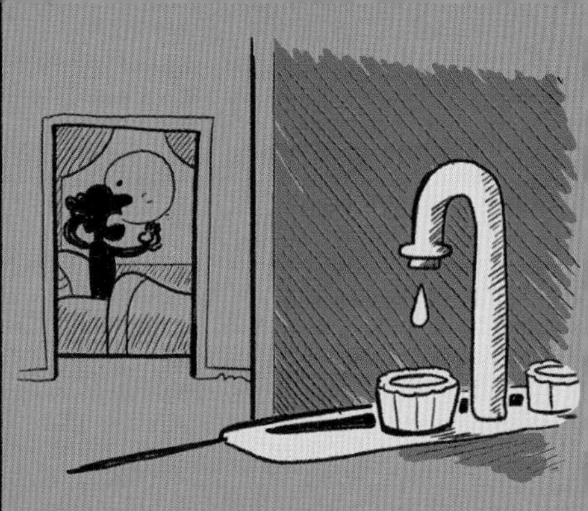

R is for Runny faucet-
it drives Dad insane!

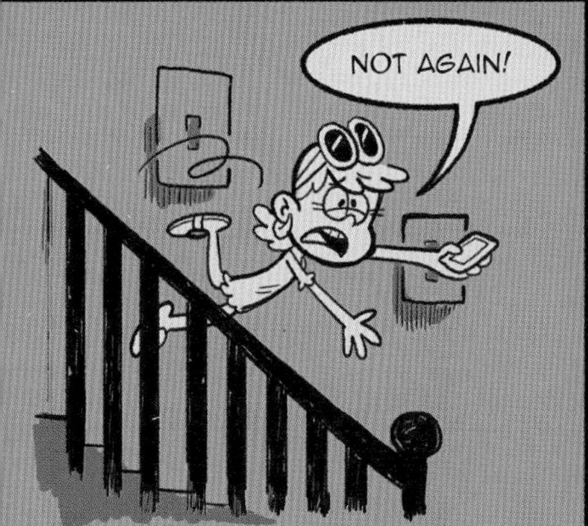
NOT AGAIN!

S is for Staircase,
where Leni pratfalls.

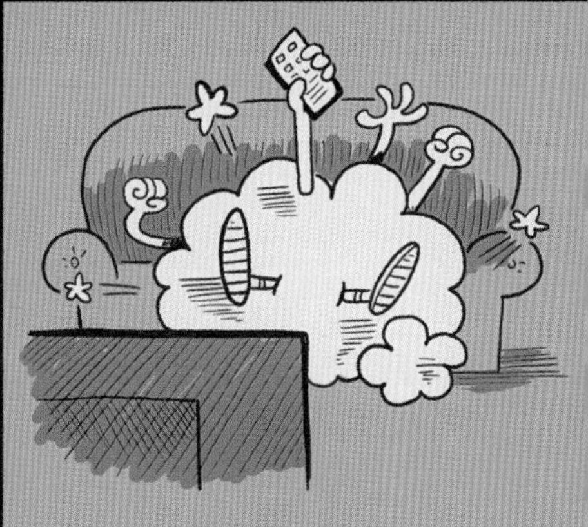

T is for TV remote,
which causes brawls.

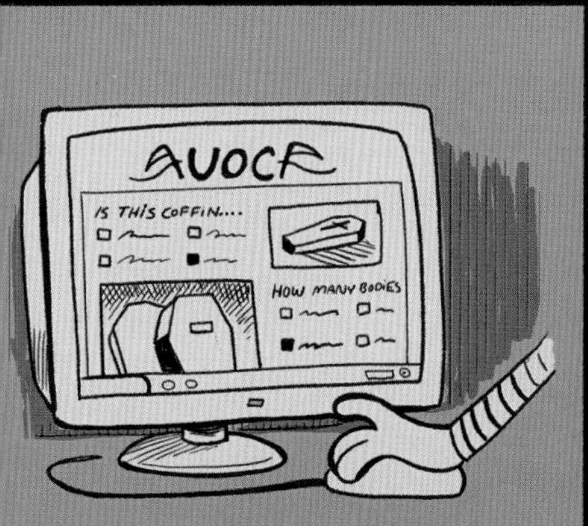
AUOCR
IS THIS COFFIN....
HOW MANY BODIES

U is for Undertaker's
online course...

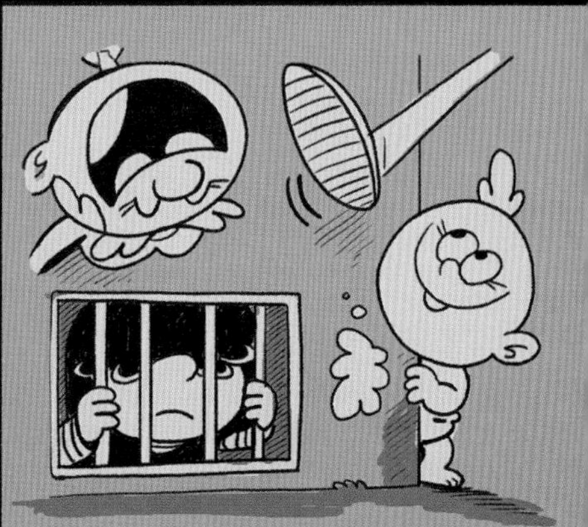

V is for Vents, when
chaos is in full force.

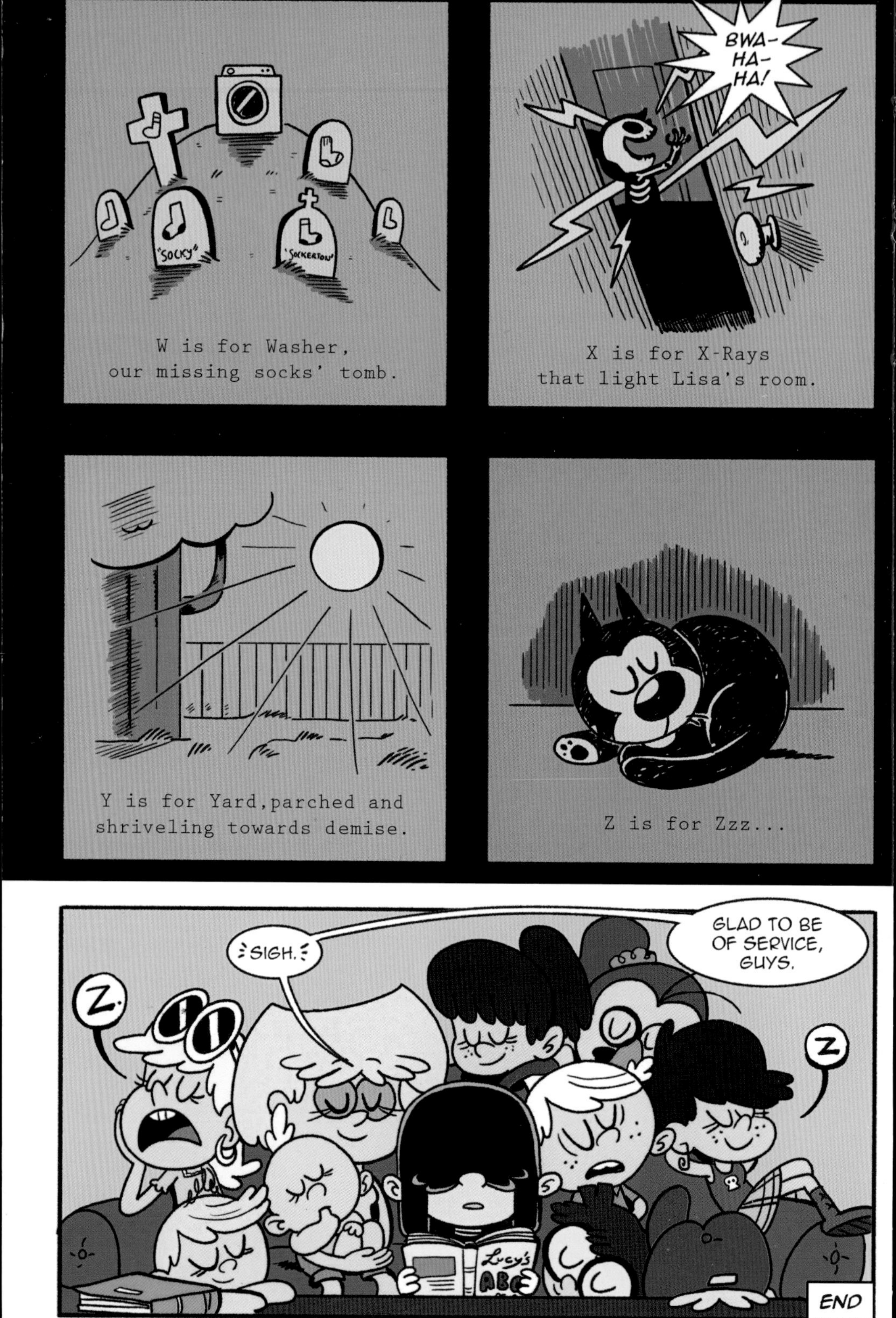
"SOCKY"
"SOCKERTON"
W is for Washer,
our missing socks' tomb.
BWA-HA-HA!
X is for X-Rays
that light Lisa's room.
Y is for Yard, parched and
shriveling towards demise.
Z is for Zzz...
Z
SIGH.
GLAD TO BE OF SERVICE, GUYS.
Z
Lucy's ABC
END

WATCH OUT FOR PAPERCUTZ

Welcome to the fourth, family-filled THE LOUD HOUSE graphic novel from Papercutz—those folks dedicated to publishing great graphic novels for all ages. I'm Jim Salicrup, the Editor-in-Chief and possessor of my very own imaginary treehouse of ideas, here with a fan letter we received from one AJ Gallucci regarding THE LOUD HOUSE. It's slightly edited for length and clarity, and I jump in throughout to offer my tree-mendous responses — so without beating around the bush, let's dig in...

Dear Mr. Salicrup,
I saw your e-mail address in THE LOUD HOUSE #1 "There Will Be Chaos" and felt I just had to write and tell you how much I loved the graphic novel.

Thanks so much, AJ! We love working with THE LOUD HOUSE and Nickelodeon to create these graphic novels. We also appreciate getting feedback here at Papercutz and hope that by publishing your comments here that other fans will share their thoughts with us as well. Let's get to the root of your letter!

The stories in "There Will Be Chaos" are definitely worthy of being turned into actual Loud House episodes. Leni is a particularly wealthy source of laugh-out loud humor. The one noticeable difference is that most of the stories in "There Will Be Chaos" are just for fun and don't have a moral as Loud House episodes often do.

The stories are mostly about funny things that have happened that may not be part of a bigger story and to focus on some of the characters besides Lincoln. What do the rest of you think? Are we barking up the wrong tree? Should we continue with short stories, switch to longer stories, or present a mix of both? Let us know. Our comics grow out of the animated series and plant an acorn in new fans who might be getting their first sampling of THE LOUD HOUSE in our graphic novels! We hope that seed will grow so everyone digging these comics blooms into full-fledged LOUD HOUSE fans!

I was captivated by the hilarious writing but it wasn't until my second reading that I truly appreciated the artwork. Not only is it as close to the artwork of the show as can be expected but it's just appealing to look at. The varying color schemes of the Loud siblings is very appealing to the eye.

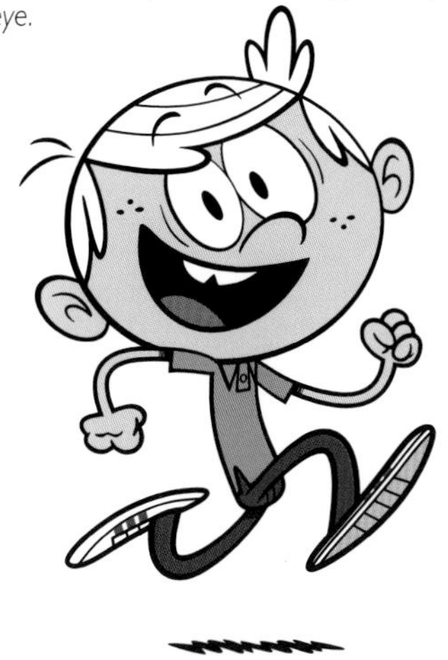

Sapling Editor Jeff Whitman very much enjoys working with the writers and artists that produce THE LOUD HOUSE TV show, and we think they enjoy working on these comics as well.

I was surprised Rita Loud doesn't appear in "There Will Be Chaos." I'm also surprised Lynn Sr. is only seen from the back. I guess either this graphic novel was developed before the show started showing the parents' faces regularly or maybe it's just because Lynn Sr. is a supporting character in a story about Lily. Hopefully future Loud House graphic novels include my favorite Loud family member: Pop Pop. The one thing I definitely want from future LOUD HOUSE graphic novels in more Luan. I know her puns are supposed to be lame but I find them as funny as heck.

It may've taken awhile, but it looks like we've included all the characters you've wanted to see in one or another of the four THE LOUD HOUSE graphic novels produced so far. We have really branched out. Here's a behind-the-scenes secret: Jeff Whitman loves supporting characters and can't resist giving each and everyone of them a little time in the spotlight. The Loud House family tree branches out in all directions, not counting the friends, family of friends, classmates, coaches, grumpy neighbors, and all the other assorted characters who've planted roots with the Louds!

Thanks again for your insightful comments, AJ, and we hope you and everyone else keep an eye out for THE LOUD HOUSE #5 this fall. In the meantime, if you're wondering what all this tree talk might be about and want to be the first to find out, I suggest you follow THE LOUD HOUSE show on Instagram at @TheLoudHouseCartoon and on Facebook.com/TheLoudHouse! Sorry to "leaf" you hanging! And of course, we at Papercutz also want to hear from you at any of the addresses below!

Excelsior!

Jim

STAY IN TOUCH!

EMAIL:	salicrup@papercutz.com
WEB:	papercutz.com
TWITTER:	@papercutzgn
INSTAGRAM:	@papercutzgn
FACEBOOK:	PAPERCUTZGRAPHICNOVELS
FANMAIL:	Papercutz, 160 Broadway, Suite 700, East Wing, New York, NY 10038

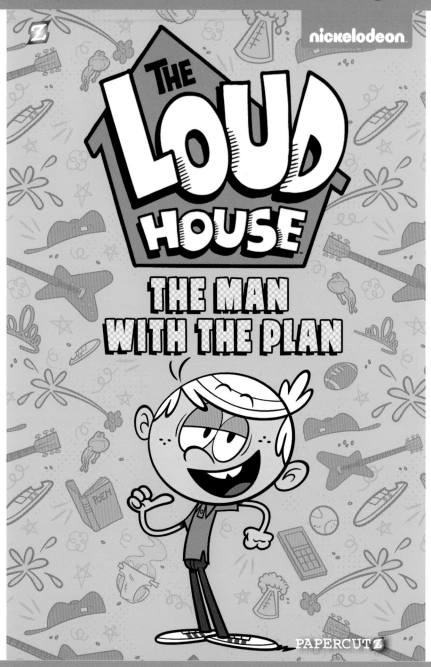